COUGAR

An Erotica Collection

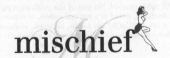

mischief

Mischief
An imprint of HarperCollins*Publishers*
77–85 Fulham Palace Road,
Hammersmith, London W6 8JB

www.mischiefbooks.com

A Paperback Original 2013

First published in Great Britain in ebook format by
HarperCollins*Publishers* 2012

A catalogue record for this book is
available from the British Library

ISBN-13: 9780007553273

Find out more about HarperCollins and the environment at
www.harpercollins.co.uk/green

CONTENTS

Contents

Pawn Shop
Lily Harlem

I glanced up from my crossword puzzle as the bell above the shop door tinkled. A man, broad shoulders, bright white smile and wearing black wraparound shades, strode into the warren of dusty shelves and cabinets. He moved with purpose, the material of his jeans hugging the tops of his long thighs and his paces eating the ground.

I'd bet my last ten quid he wasn't from around here. Fenchurch Brokers had been my home from home since I was a young girl and I'd taken it over when Pops had died ten years ago. I knew everyone's face, the way they knew mine.

'So what have you got for me?' I asked, then realised a few moments too late that I'd fluffed my brunette locks over my shoulders and licked my lips.

His broadening grin told me he was used to the effect he had on women, of any age.

Inwardly I berated myself. I was the local bank-of-crisis, get-money-quick supplier. I bought crap, or treasure, for pennies, and sold it on for a few quid whenever red letters landed on doormats or kitchen cupboards were bare. I didn't do the whole simpering female thing. That just wasn't me.

'DVDs,' he said and dumped a dark-green carrier bag on the counter.

'Not much call for them, I'm afraid.' I sighed, trying to feign nonchalance. 'What kind of films are they?' I put down the pen I was holding, to keep me from tapping it on the counter.

He shoved his hands into the pockets of his jeans and rocked back on his heels. 'This is a pawnshop, right?'

'Yes.' His cologne was wafting towards me – tropical breeze and fresh open water. It seeped up my nostrils, sped up my pulse and created a tickle of sensation around my temples.

Damn.

'So I can sell you these, for cash,' he went on, 'and if I decide I want them back, and they're still in the shop, I can repurchase them?'

'That's generally how it works.' I noticed that his bottom lip was fuller than the top and had the tiniest indentation in the centre. To my annoyance I found myself utterly mesmerised by it and unable to tear my attention away from his mouth.

'Great.' He pushed the bag nearer to me. 'Because I don't need these anymore, I've watched them all. But I'd like the chance of getting them back if I can at some stage.'

Standing, I smoothed my skirt and glanced at my displayed cleavage. Today I wore a low-buttoned, silky-black blouse and a string of pearls. 'Are they recent movies?'

'Yeah, all from the last year.' He cocked his head and grinned, his gaze following mine and leaving a heated trail down my throat and over my chest.

I withdrew the first DVD from the bag. *Full of Tristan.* On the front was a picture of two naked guys standing facing out to sea, one with his hand on the other's arse.

'They're not conventional blockbusters,' he said. 'More of a speciality, you know, collectors' editions.'

I frowned and pulled out the next one. *The Gardener's Best Tool. I* studied the cover: a large green bush strewn with underwear, from behind the foliage two pairs of feet stuck out in such a way it was obvious what the couple were doing.

He leaned forward on the counter, placed his elbows at points and rested his chin on his clasped hands. 'I understand if they're not your thing,' he said then bit down on his bottom lip, flattening out that delectable dink. 'Some people just can't cope with porn, especially older generations.'

The hairs on the back of my neck bristled. What

the hell did he think I was? Some old lady about to get shipped off to the nursing home with nothing more to look forward to than *Strictly* on a Saturday night? Cheeky bugger!

'I don't have a problem with porn,' I said, casually stacking the DVDs on top of one another and counting them with a neutral expression on my face. Eighteen in total.

He lifted his shades, propped them on his head. His irises were an interesting mix of hazel and green and reminded me of melting mint-choc-chip ice-cream.

'You don't?' he asked, raising his brows.

'No.' Small drops of sweat popped on my cleavage as his eyes twinkled. Damn it, why was I letting some gorgeous young man get to me this way? I was Nadia Fenchurch – no one got to me.

'So how much will you give me for them?' he asked, touching a small silver cross that sat in the hollow of his throat.

'Well, there are eighteen, I reckon I'll sell them on for just a few quid each, so twelve pounds the lot.'

He raised his brows. 'That's not much, hardly worth the bother.'

I shrugged. 'You want an extra few bob in your pocket or what?'

'Barely get me a couple of pints.'

'Better than giving them away.'

4

'Mmm.' One side of his mouth twitched into a half-smile.

I reached for his empty carrier bag and set about smoothing it and folding it. A completely unnecessary task but I had to do something to engage my fiddling fingers.

'I suppose it will be interesting,' he said.

'What will be?'

'To give them to you.' He dropped his shades down over his eyes again.

'What does that mean?'

He shrugged, in a maddeningly sexy kind of way that made me want to slap him and lick him all at the same time. 'Nothing, I didn't mean anything by it. Can I get my cash?'

I opened my ancient vinegar-brown till and plucked out a note and a couple of coins. 'Here you go.' I passed him the money and for a second our hands connected. The briefest of moments when heat from his flesh seeped into mine and created a sizzle of sensation up my arm. It had been a long time since I'd touched a handsome man and every erogenous zone in my body went on full alert.

But the connection was over in an instant and he turned, weaved past a table of odds-and-sods and a selection of old TVs and disappeared out onto the street.

I sat with a bump and fanned my face with my puzzle book. Phew, he was a hottie. If I was ten years younger, he'd have been just my cup of tea for getting naked, sweaty and down and dirty with.

After nipping into the backroom for a glass of water, I set about sorting the DVDs. They were all pornographic with a variety of either lewd or suggestive covers. I couldn't remember the last time I'd watched something explicit, and as I set them out on a high shelf behind the till I wondered if I might borrow one, take it home and remind myself of what a good fuck looked like.

Full of Tristan didn't appeal, though *The Gardener's Best Tool* was a possibility. I sifted through the other titles, *Spanked*, *The Blushing Bride's Darkest Desire*, *His Best Performance*. Which one to choose?

The male on the cover of *His Best Performance* caught my eye. Tall, dark hair, sensual mouth with an indentation in his bottom lip.

No way.

Bloody hell, was it him? My hot customer!

It couldn't be.

I studied the cover more closely. It absolutely, definitely was him. Those eyes, high cheekbones, broad shoulders. OK, I'd seen him fully clothed and on the cover of *His Best Performance* he wore only a pair of swimming trunks – tiny, tight, yellow – but I recognised him beyond doubt. I swallowed a lump in my throat. What was beneath his clothes was nothing short of beautiful. Golden chest,

6

defined abs and a tantalising trail of hair from his naval to the waistband of those itsy-bitsy trunks.

Behind him a woman reclined on a sun-lounger, her arms tossed above her head and a towel carefully placed on her naked body to cover the juncture of her thighs, though her full breasts jutted towards the sun. She was the picture of bliss with her eyes shut, back arched and parted mouth upturned in a smile. He'd obviously used the cock I could just decipher the outline of, to give her exactly what she wanted and then some.

My heart thudded. I could hear my pulse whooshing through my ears. I glanced at the door half expecting to see him watching me through the glass.

He wasn't.

Without another moment's hesitation, I slipped the DVD into my handbag between my purse and a paperback. There was no competition as to which porn film I would be taking home tonight. It could only be *His Best Performance*. I just hoped it lived up to my expectations.

I glanced at a grandfather clock I'd been trying to sell for three years. Good, it was nearly time to shut up. A heat was flooding my pelvis and my nipples were tingling. For once I was looking forward to something other than *EastEnders* on the TV tonight.

* * *

I re-checked there wasn't a crack in my curtains and hit play on the remote. My darkened living room flooded with light. The movie prelude was a bright sun rising from a black horizon. I skipped forward a few frames. The movie began and I was deafened by a piano tune that accompanied crashing waves.

After turning down the volume, I took a sip of my drink. The gin was sharp on my tongue, a delicious bitter assault on my tastebuds. I was all about my senses tonight. I was hoping Jared – I knew his name now, it was written in bold letters across the top of the box: 'starring Jared Letterman'– would give me a little bit of the experience that naked pool lady had enjoyed.

The movie started, a set-up about a rich but bored woman with a movie-executive husband. Jared – in the movie he's known as Dirk – turned up for an audition at her lavish Hollywood home only to find the husband out at work.

Within minutes the action was getting steamy. I gulped at my drink and shrugged out of my cardigan as Jared stepped out of his jeans. Seeing his naked body did funny things to my insides; they were tumbling and heating, swelling with a hunger for something I'd lived without for too many years.

Before long, the glamorous wife and Jared were shagging. At first in the pool, then the hot tub, and finally they performed oral sex on each other on the lounger which led to her riding him like a world rodeo champion.

I stared at his face, his cock, the rippling muscles on his back and buttocks as he threw himself into his tasks. He was perfection, every single inch of him exactly how a man should be. As the film came to an end – Jared being offered the starring role in the next big blockbuster by her unwitting husband – I found I'd slipped my fingers beneath the waistband of my skirt.

A need had grown, a desire for pressure and stimulation. My breaths were coming quick and as I pressed on my clit my knees flopped open and my butt-cheeks tensed. Quickly I rewound to the sun-lounger scene, Jared licking the woman's pussy, making her squirm and squeal and clutch at his hair. Staring, unblinking, I imagined it was me that he was fucking with his tongue, just like that.

Rotating my fingers, I canted my hips upwards. I wasn't gentle; this was about satisfaction and letting my imagination fly me away on a wonderful fantasy. To have a man as insanely beautiful and talented as Jared sucking on my clit, thrusting his fingers into my pussy, was an image that had given me wings.

Soon I was coming, just as the woman on TV shouted that she was in her loud American voice. I upped the speed and gripped my left breast with my free hand, the way Jared was doing to her.

I spiralled into bliss, my clit throbbing and pulsing. I wanted to shut my eyes, close in on myself, but I didn't.

Instead, I kept them wide open, staring straight at Jared as he slowed his ministrations and wiped his forearm over his shiny mouth.

'Oh, oh,' I panted, slipping down the armchair a little. My spine like dust, my thighs trembling.

But only one thing was going through my mind.

Had he meant to leave that DVD in my shop?

* * *

The next morning business was quiet. An elderly gentleman enquired about the grandfather clock but grunted when I told him the price. A woman who visited regularly with fine pieces of jewellery accepted thirty pounds for a gold bracelet with a butterfly clasp. She gripped the notes, her eyes moist and her lips a tight line. I decided to put the bracelet to the back of the cabinet so only the most observant of punters would spot it, then gave the little girl standing quietly at her side a mint from my jar.

I was just about to switch the sign at the front of the shop to CLOSED and retreat to my back room for a cheese sandwich and a Cup-a-Soup when the door opened.

'I'm shut for an hour,' I called, my head still dipped over the glass-topped drawer.

'So do you want me to flip this sign for you?'

A flush swarmed over my chest and up my neck. I would recognise that voice anywhere. Especially after listening to him on my TV last night.

I shut the drawer and straightened, trying to look unflustered. Then watched Jared flip the cardboard sign hanging on a piece of putty so it read OPEN to the inside of the shop.

'What do you want?' I asked, heat travelling over my scalp and flaming onto my cheeks.

He sauntered up to the desk, removing his shades and poking them into the 'v' neckline of his black T-shirt. 'I need to buy one of my DVDs back. It shouldn't have been in the pile.'

'Well, I'm afraid you'll have to come back later. I'm closed now, for lunch.'

'But it won't take a minute. It's the one called *His Best Performance*.' He tipped his head and studied the shelf behind me.

Shit.

The DVD he wanted was still in my player at home. I'd had plans to watch it again, later, after a hot bath and with a dildo that had been gathering dust of late.

'Mmm,' he said, rubbing his bottom lip with his index finger. 'I can't see it.'

My mind whirred. I struggled to think straight. 'I sold it. Someone bought it, this morning.'

His sharp gaze caught mine and he gave me that look

11

again, the one that made me feel like he was seeing right inside me. 'Really?'

'Yes, really.' I fiddled with a string of red beads around my neck, looping them in and out of my fingers.

'That's an odd coincidence.'

'Why is it? Someone came in, they wanted porn, that's what they bought.'

'Male or female?'

'I, um, male, not that it matters.'

He lifted his finger and made a show of counting the remaining DVDs, mouthing the numbers as he did so. 'And he just bought one?'

'Yes.'

He sighed and rested a black leather jacket over the counter. 'Fuck, that's a real pity.'

I licked my lips and studied the cross that was wedged at a slight angle at the base of his throat. I couldn't help but wonder what his flesh would taste like there, what it would feel like on the tip of my tongue. A little rough in texture but a sweet flavour that matched the way he smelled. 'Why does it matter?' I asked.

'Because it was important to me.'

I just bet it was.

'There's nothing I can do, Jared, it's gone out into the big wide world, never to return.' As I spoke my stomach dropped. Panic swam through my veins and my breath stuttered in my throat.

Fuck.

He raised his brows and straightened. 'How do you know my name?'

I stopped fiddling with my necklace, crossed my arms and balled my fists.

'How do you know my name?' he asked again, cocking his head.

'I'm shut for lunch. Please leave and come back another time if you want to repurchase your DVDs.' I turned and went into the sanctuary of my backroom. My legs were wobbly, my knees weak, but I held my chin high.

I gasped when there was a sudden tightening on my right upper arm.

'You watched it, didn't you?' Jared spun me to face him. 'You didn't sell it, you kept it for yourself. That's how you know my name.'

'Don't be so ridiculous.' He didn't look angry; instead he looked pleased, triumphant almost.

'So tell me, what did you think of my performance?'

I stepped backwards and he followed, holding both my upper arms now. My shoulders hit the wall and he pressed his body against mine and looked down at me. His face was so close I could make out a small scar just below his left eye and see every dark eyelash individually.

'I don't know what you mean,' I said, acutely aware of his hard pecs shoved up against the soft mounds of my breasts. Pushing, pressing into me.

'Quit the games,' he said with a slow smile. 'You watched me in action, you loved it, it turned you on.' His voice was low and rumbling, and it did funny things to the very pit of my stomach.

'No, I didn't.' My denial was feeble, even to my ears.

Suddenly his mouth was on mine, hard, urgent and dominant.

I gasped a protest and smacked my fists against his solid body. But he ignored me and plundered my mouth with his tongue, feeding me his syrupy yet raw flavour.

My protest turned into a groan of delight and I scrabbled for his shoulders, barely knowing whether to shove him away or drag him closer for more.

God, the man could kiss. Not only that, he was kissing me like he really was enjoying it, not acting, but actually wanted me.

He ran his hands up my arms, over my shoulders and cradled my face. 'You're fucking gorgeous,' he whispered onto my lips.

If I could have let go of him to pinch myself and make sure I wasn't dreaming, I would have. 'Really?'

'Yes, really.'

'But surely you can have anyone, any young bimbo you want.'

'For the record, bimbos don't do it for me. I like an independent woman who knows who she is, what she wants and isn't afraid to work for it.'

14

'And that's me?'

'Too damn right it is.' He kissed over my cheek, settled his lips at the shell of my ear. His breaths were hot and hard, like a storm blowing right through me.

'So tell me,' he said, pulling back just far enough to look at my face. 'Which was your favourite part of the movie? What did I do best?'

'I, well … I'm …'

'Quit pretending you didn't watch it, because I know a hot-blooded woman like you wouldn't have been able to resist.'

OK, I was rumbled and, let's face it, I'd only watched the movie – he was the bloody star of it. What did it matter if I confessed to having seen it?

I wound my hands up and over his shoulders and linked my fingers at his nape. Pulled in a deep breath laced with his intoxicating cologne, and harnessed my courage. 'I liked it when you fucked her with your mouth.'

He grinned. It was kind of an arrogant tilt to his lips, but at the same time so damn sexy my pussy actually trembled.

'Yeah, that's a speciality of mine,' he said.

Suddenly he dropped to his knees and I was left looking at the top of his head, studying the little whirl of hair at his crown.

He slid his hands upwards, scooping my skirt and letting the material gather at his wrists.

'Jesus,' I said. 'Anyone could come in and see you doing that.' I glanced at the door.

He reached and placed his palm on the wood. Shoved it so hard the door slammed shut with an ear-splitting bang, and a framed picture of dogs playing pool shifted on its nail. 'There, now your skirt has no need to fear being caught *inflagrante delicto*.' As he spoke he slid it right up, so that it sat like a belt at my waist.

'Jared,' I gasped. 'What are you doing?'

He looked at me, licked his lips and grinned. 'I'm going to give you a personal demonstration of my best performance.'

If my knees had been weak before, now they were positively noodle-like. What the hell was I doing? Could I really let this gorgeous young man go down on me in the back of my shop?

Like hell I could.

He tugged my knickers below my knees and eased apart my thighs. Pressed his mouth to my lower abdomen, softly, reverently, the light sprinkle of stubble on his chin slightly scratchy.

A juddering sigh escaped my lips and I slotted my hands into the thick, warm strands of his hair. Letting it mesh around my fingers and tickle my knuckles.

His attentions headed south and he kissed through my patch of pubic hair, tugging the roots slightly and creating a tingling sensation that travelled straight to my clit.

'Mmm, you smell divine,' he murmured, burrowing his nose further in and nuzzling it side to side. He pulled in a deep breath, his shoulders shifting as his chest expanded.

'Oh, God,' I said. The erotic image of him filling his lungs up with my scent was almost enough to make me come right then.

'You smell of woman and desire,' he said, sliding his hands up and down my thighs, hips to knees, knees to hips. 'Perfect.'

Suddenly he ducked and arrowed his tongue through my soft folds, lapping and swooping, almost urgently.

'Ah, ah.' Pleasure shot through me. Pleasure and disbelief and, as he said, desire. I could feel my pussy dampening, a hot wetness seeping from me. And he was lapping at it eagerly. Groaning his approval as he did so. His warm, firm tongue was divine on flesh that had been neglected for so long. Searching and stimulating, drinking from me as though I was a honeyed treat.

I tightened my grip on his head and parted my legs further, giving him unhindered access.

Another few seconds and he found my clit.

'Oh, God,' I said panting. My knees buckled. I struggled to remain upright and was glad of the support of the wall behind me.

He was exploring my right inner thigh with his fingertips, winding upward, stroking and caressing. My pussy clenched; it felt like a gaping hole that needed filling.

17

Jared must have sensed my need because his fingers circled my entrance, spreading my moisture around, teasing and fondling.

'Please,' I murmured, 'oh, please, inside.'

He stretched my pussy with his big long fingers, two at least pushing in, easing me open.

My spine curled and I squeezed my eyes shut, gripped him with my internal muscles. Electric whips of sensation burned through my core. He was working me with his tongue, fucking me with his fingers. For a moment I imagined I was that beautiful woman on the DVD being serviced as I lounged by a pool in the sunshine. I was glamorous and rich and living in LA. My body young and lithe, my skin flawless and smooth. Thinking nothing of wearing a bikini from dawn to dusk.

And the Californian sun could well have been heating me, for my body was feverish, sex-sweat pricking at my flesh. The blistering pressure was growing and building. I gripped his hair and thrust my hips in time with his penetrations. Forgot about that woman in the sun and became me again. The star of my own smokin' porn movie with Jared as my co-star.

'Oh, God, I'm going to come,' I moaned, throwing my head back against the wall and staring up at the dusty lampshade.

He reached up and grabbed my breast, squeezed and massaged, plucked at my nipple through my blouse and bra.

The nip of pain tipped me over the edge. I was there, teetering on the precipice of an almighty orgasm. So much better than any at my own hand. My breath caught, my heart thudded, every muscle in my body tensed.

He shunted into me even higher, sped up the rotations over my swollen clit and palmed my breast in a big hard grab.

Bliss flooded my soul, my torso slumped forward and my pussy gripped and spasmed around his fingers. A cry echoed around the room and it wasn't until the tail-end of the noise that I realised it came from me.

Jared stayed with me, expertly working my pussy, carrying me to the end of my climax and then bringing me gently down.

My breaths were hard to catch and moisture popped all over my body. I could barely focus on his features when he finally stood and withdrew his fingers. My vision was blurry, my brain in a dazed state.

He grinned and wiped his shiny mouth on the back of his hand. I caught a whiff of my arousal – my come.

'So,' he said.

'So what?' I reached for his upper arms and fisted his T-shirt, needing the extra support for my floaty body.

'Was that my best performance?'

I grinned and then giggled, quite giddily. 'Definitely, as far as I'm concerned.' His handsome face came back into focus. He was flushed, his lips a little puffy and the skin around them pink and moist.

'Good.' He dropped a musky kiss onto my mouth then stepped away, forcing me to release him.

Instantly I felt cool, the loss of his body heat like a cold draught. I shivered and failed to suppress a final blissful tremor as it wound up my spine.

Reality hit. Hurriedly I pulled up my knickers and straightened out my skirt. Shoved my hair behind my ears and realigned my bra and beads. How I must look I had no idea.

Jared reached for the door handle, his movements as smooth and graceful as ever. 'So do you think you could bring the DVD in for me tomorrow?'

'I, um, sure. Of course.'

He walked out of view. 'Jared,' I called, tottering forward, my quivering thighs only just doing as instructed. 'I, but … I mean … why?'

He grabbed his jacket and turned, reached for his shades. 'Why what?'

'Why did you, you know, just then, do that?'

His gaze latched onto mine. 'Let's just say I like to keep my fans happy and you, Miss Fenchurch, are someone I've always wanted to make happy.'

Confusion wriggled through my mind. I clutched my necklace and twisted it like a rosary. Trying desperately to figure out the puzzle. 'You say that like you've known me for a long time.'

He pointed to the jar of mint humbugs next to the till.

'When I was a kid you used to give me a sweet whenever you helped out my mam, which was a lot.'

'Your mam?'

'Petunia Kirkwood.'

'Oh, Petunia, yes, of course.' I dropped the beads and clasped my hands to my mouth. 'Bloody hell, you're little Johnny Kirkwood? I would never have – God, it's been so long since your mam told me you were heading to LA with stars in your eyes.'

'Yeah, I guess it has been a while.' He slotted his shades on and opened the shop door. The bell tinkled as a self-satisfied grin spread on his face.' I'll see you tomorrow then,' he said.

And just like that little Johnny Kirkwood, who was not so little any more, was gone.

Sighing I sat on my chair, my nether regions swollen and damp. I couldn't help but wonder if tomorrow, when he came back for his porn, there might be a repeat performance.

And, if that was a possibility, I would have to watch the movie all over again, just in case he asked if I had another favourite scene and offered me a personal performance.

B and B
Primula Bond

My friends swore I'd be bored stiff in the countryside. A year ago Soho was my stomping ground. Bars and clubs my natural habitat. Conference calls my mode of communication. But a girl can get tired of the stress and grime, tube trains and flight paths, impossible deadlines and demanding clients.

One-night stands were my sex life, fuelled by frustration, wine and the potential for danger. But a girl can tire of thumping hangovers and meaningless fucking, especially when she hits forty.

So when my fairy godmother bequeathed me her chocolate-box cottage and thriving bed-and-breakfast business I shocked everyone by upping sticks and moving to Camber Sands. People even laid bets on how soon I'd tire of green fields, oast houses, gossiping neighbours and the slow grey roll of the English Channel.

The arrival of a slick, single city girl in a village full of retirees and young families certainly wasn't greeted with fanfare. I stuck out like a sore thumb with my red lippy and loud laugh, my vociferous reluctance to bake cakes or join the flower rota. I was viewed with suspicion as I struggled to keep my godmother's hollyhocks and roses going, the tourists arriving and the husbands at arm's length.

But when the London gang turned up unannounced on the first anniversary of my move they didn't find me alone and palely knitting. Oh no. They found themselves gate-crashing a raucous gathering of apple-cheeked locals singing along to *X Factor* and getting rat-arsed on my vodka cocktails.

'Us backwater types thought Sara was like the woman from that film, *Chocolat*, springing from nowhere,' the vicar, who also teaches street dancing in the school hall, confided once my shell-shocked mates were parked in the inglenook fireplace. 'She was like a beautiful alien, but now you can't keep people away.'

'It's a mystery,' my friends muttered later as they piled back into their Lexus because there was no room at the inn. 'I guess you can take the career girl out of London, but you can't take London out of the career girl.'

Like the meerkat says – *simples*. People flock here because I give them what they want. So, not only the extra draw of a studio and painting tuition for budding artists, but also food, and lots of it. People have to eat, don't they, especially on holiday? As well as all-day breakfast, I do a wicked cream tea. And people have to drink. My garden bar is full every evening, cosy in winter, out on the terrace last summer.

They have to sleep, don't they? I've got rooms. Exposed beams, four-posters, chintz. Everything you'd want from a chic B and B off the beaten track. And since the summer, when it was mostly families, there's been a rash of youngsters, art students arriving in groups. Boys, mostly, the odd smattering of girls. Word of mouth apparently, and my inviting website. They come here to get away from parents, from college. They come to learn to paint. To get stoned. Oh, and they come here to –

'By the way,' my ex-secretary shouted as the car pulled away. 'Where did you find the young hunk handing round the cocktails?'

– get laid. I was going to say they come here to get laid.

Forget the bastards I left behind in London, the hungry husbands I have to fend off here. What I've discovered down here is boys. Old enough to have driving licences, obviously – hell, what do you take me for? – but still cute, fresh-faced, uncomplicated. They don't want much at that age. Just food, friends, sleep and sex. They're permanently hard at that age, aren't they? Permanently ready. And permanently grateful.

So where did I find my young hunk? Sniffing my knickers.

It was a breezy autumnal afternoon and I was prowling about in an old maxi skirt and flowery blouse tied round my middle, watering, cleaning, cooking, rearranging the art work. The students had gone to the sand dunes to paint the sea birds.

Except someone was in my garden, fingering my washing. A tall boy I'd seen earlier. I stepped out on to the wet grass, poking my bare toes through the rustling leaves just as he lifted my knickers to his face and inhaled.

'Oh, God! Didn't know anyone was there. Got left behind.'

Such a deep voice. Such a deep blush.

'I can drive you down to the beach to find the others.'

I swayed towards him, cold air whistling over my skin where my shirt was unbuttoned. I'd got hot while baking scones.

'Rather stay here. Didn't feel too good.' He was breathing hard and staring straight at my breasts, bulging in their dark-pink bra. He yanked his jeans up by the waistband, but not quickly enough to hide the outline of his prick, which was trying to stand straight up in his pants.

I came closer and laid my hand on his forehead.

'Maybe you should have a lie-down.'

His face was so smooth, golden spikes of stubble pushing through his chin and cheeks. He swallowed, his Adam's apple jumping. He could easily shove me away

25

but he glanced up, brown eyes smouldering. Quarter boy, three-quarters man.

It had been nearly a year since I'd been fucked. I wanted him, badly. But he was a punter. And I have an open-house policy. Anyone could walk into this garden.

As I was about to turn into the house, he lifted his hand, pushed my blouse to one side, and touched my left breast. It was juddering with my crazy heartbeat. He moved his hand over the lace. I laid my hand over his to show him I liked it. He pressed harder. Then I licked my finger, ran it down the crack of my cleavage, stroked the soft swell, then pushed the bra down to expose my breast and to show him how my finger, wet from my mouth, was teasing my nipple.

He followed the movement, so now his finger was inside my bra, too. He circled that nipple, then hooked his thumb over the bra to push it down. Now they were both out, proud, tingling in the cold air. Nipples stiff as nuts to show him my excitement.

I came to my senses and walked into the house, pulling my blouse closed.

'I think maybe I do need that lie-down,' he croaked behind me.

Desire stirred in my belly. Think quickly, but carefully.

'More peaceful up in my room,' I murmured, rearranging some lilies in a vase. 'I mean, in case the others come crashing back and disturb you.'

26

I started to walk up the crooked little staircase that leads only to my own private quarters.

'All women should be motherly, and sexy, like you.'

I started to blush like a schoolgirl and laughed, much too loudly. I nonchalantly opened the door to my private quarters.

'I could put you across my knee for saying things like that, boyo.'

'I'd much rather take you across mine.'

Wow. These boy-men have a way of pulling the rug out from under you. One minute helpless babies, the next coming on like a practised lothario. The way he said it, his voice so low and rough and rude, was all the more thrilling for being so unexpected.

I responded in the best way I know, which was to beckon him into my bedroom under the eaves.

My B and B is immaculate, but from the mess you'd think a slut lived in the attic. And you'd be right.

By now I was creaming for him. My breasts were aching to be sucked, nipples hardening just thinking about it. I didn't know if he was following me, but still I checked my reflection. I looked like a gypsy. My hair had fallen in messy ringlets round my flushed face.

I wriggled out of my skirt, let it drop to the floor, and there he was, behind me in the mirror. My hunk walking right into my bedroom and flinging himself down on the sofa.

'You said I could lie down?'

I nodded, swaying towards him. A button popped comically off my blouse as if unable to contain itself, or my cleavage. He was right there, his hands on my buttocks, pulling me against him. His nose pushed into the soft give of my pussy lips, barely concealed under my silky knickers, and I parted my legs a little. He closed his eyes and sniffed at my pussy, then ripped the tiny knickers off with his teeth. Three-quarters man, one quarter boy. Then I felt the tip of his wet tongue. Like he was striking a match on my clit.

I froze, but he mistook my silence and hesitated. I gently touched the top of his head, and that was it. He grabbed me round the waist and tumbled me on top of him. I landed, skin on skin, my blouse dropping off my shoulders like falling petals, and now I could feel all the warmth of his gorgeous young body spread out under me but mostly the battering of his heart and the urgent hardening of his cock inside his jeans.

I tried to land on my hands and catch my own weight, rather than knock my elbows into his face and ruin the moment, but it was my breasts that fell forwards, bouncing against his face. I languished for a moment, then raised myself up to look at him.

He was mine. All mine. My prize on a cold, lazy day. A feast of young manhood laid out on my sofa, comfortable as you like, not going anywhere, any doubts knocked out of the ring by the force of his lust. I was rubbing myself against him without knowing it, hungry to get him inside me. Everything about him was irresistible, his eyes, his full lips, the little bubbles of saliva at the corners like a kid impatient to tell you something, the pulse pummelling in his tanned neck.

And that big young cock barging up in his shorts. Any minute now, at a time I was going to choose, I was going to have a damn good look at it. I was going to touch it, hold it. I wouldn't be able to help myself sliding on to it –

It makes me horny even now, can you tell? Remembering the sight of him, the smell, the heat burning off him that first time. I wasn't his first, but I was going to make sure he'd never forget me.

'Oh, my God, those tits, good enough to eat. Oh, God, I want to fuck you.'

I cupped my breasts, massaged them together, licking my lips like a porn star. 'You seen breasts like mine before? Full, generous, begging to be touched?'

He shook his head, watching me fondle myself.

'Different, aren't they?' I whispered. I was chancing it, but I knew he was hooked. His little girlie friends would have cute white baps. Not even a handful each.

'Dark, aren't they?' I said softly, leaning nearer, dangling them over him, juicy like fruit. My nipples had turned the colour of raspberries. He couldn't take his eyes off them. They were inches from his mouth and lips and tongue and teeth. I wanted him to suck me. The tension was so electric you could hear it.

I arched my back to thrust my breasts towards him. His Adam's apple jumped again. His hands came up from my hips, where they'd tried to steady me in falling, and slid up my ribcage until they reached the outward curve of my breasts. I breathed in tiny gasps as his hands slid closer. The room was so quiet. His body was straining up under me. My nipples were stiff and burning, each one now the size of the tip of his little finger.

'Let me,' he groaned. I rubbed one across his mouth. I felt as if I'd been punched in the stomach. His face flooded with red heat. Did he flush like that with his little floozies? Did he get rushes of excitement when they gave him a flash? Or a full-on erection like the one banging out of his jeans right now?

I let my nipples hover just above his mouth, torturing us both. I ran my hand over the front of his jeans, felt the rigid outline. I reached inside to cup his warm balls.

Outside it was getting dark. The kettle needed boiling. The guests would be back soon from the beach.

I picked up one of his hands, placed it on one swollen breast. My nipple spiked up, poking against his palm. I went limp as his fingers closed round. I spread my knees to lower myself, my pussy opening, my breasts jumping into his face with each heartbeat.

30

I had a boy here with the body of a god, just waiting for me to show him. So much for being bored in the countryside.

My stomach tightened as he played with both breasts, moulded them, squeezed until I could bear it no longer. I lay on him, smothering him, so that he had no choice but to nuzzle in between, press each breast against each of his hot cheeks. I took one breast, so heavy with wanting, and rubbed the taut nipple against his mouth again and again. Just the sight of me holding it, offering it to him, made me want to come. I jammed myself against his legs, but my pussy was twitching with frustration.

His tongue flicked out and I angled the tit right into his mouth. His lips nibbled up, tongue lapping round, then, aah, at last, he drew the burning bud in, pulling hard, and began to suck. Sparks pricked at me. I looked down at his tousled hair, at the salt water dried in granules and flecked white across his cheekbones, and I closed my eyes as the sensation nearly finished me off.

He brought the other breast up and turned his head this way and that, lapping and sucking, snuffling through his nose to breathe, groaning, biting and kneading harder and harder as if he owned my breasts now. It wasn't enough for one breast to be suckled, they both had to be. That's what really does it for me. Suck one, pinch the other until they're both singing with pain. So the harder I pushed into his face, the quicker he learned, the harder he bit and chewed and pinched, and the sharper my pleasure.

'Fuck me,' a woman howled, and it was me.

'Show me,' he grunted back.

I wanted him to go on and on sucking and biting my tits, but I wanted his stiff cock in my cunt, too, wanted to feel it ramming up me. But somehow I still kept it slow. I wanted him to remember every single move.

I planted my knees on either side of his thighs so I was straddling him, still crushing his head between my tits, still making him suck. I wanted him to suck and suck forever, except that soon I would come against his leg like some randy bitch and what sort of education would that be?

As my nipples burned and throbbed, I rolled his jeans and boxers down. He raised his hips so obligingly to let me undress him I wanted to weep with victory. And then I wanted to shriek with it when his cock came thumping out from the rough tangle of tawny curls, pulsating like the rest of him, its surface smooth like velvet.

God, anyone would think I'd never seen one before. It thumped all heavy and warm into my hand and its owner bit me, hard, so that I screamed out loud.

'You're a quick learner,' I breathed, pulling away, letting his head follow me, still nibbling and biting. 'So here's a little reward.'

He fell back, mouth wet with licking, and I slithered down till I reached his dick, standing there like a beacon.

The tip was already beading. If I wasn't careful, he'd come like a bloody train, before I wanted him to. But I wanted to show him. So I took that boy's cock right into my mouth until the knob knocked the back of my throat.

His buttocks clenched as I sucked on him, holding his balls and biting my way down his shaft and sucking the sweet length of it. He started bucking. I wanted him to think he'd died and gone to heaven. Any minute now I was going to heaven, too. As I sucked, I rubbed my aching tits and wet pussy up and down his legs, like a randy mare scratching against a fence. He pulled at my hair. I was in danger of wasting this golden moment by coming all over his shins. My pussy was convulsing frantically now, leaving a slick of juice on his legs.

I gave his dick one last, long suck, pulling it and nipping it, then I let it slide out past my teeth. Next time I'd swallow. I clambered back on top of him, my toy, my boy, as he started to rise up on his elbows, seeking my tits again. I tilted myself over him.

'See how beautiful it is,' I crooned at him, showing him his cock in my fingers, wet with my licking. 'See how well it's going to fit.'

I aimed the tip of his cock towards my bush, let it rest there, nudge into my wet lips, and I shuddered as each inch went in. The tension was ecstasy, but I was going wild here, especially when he grabbed my breasts and started sucking on them again. I couldn't hold on to it for much longer, and I let the boy's knob slide up inside, all the way to the hilt. It was tempting to ram it, but once it was right in I forced myself away again.

'Let me fuck you!'

We'd lost the power of language. 'Fuck' was the only word we knew.

I moaned in reply, tossed my head back, and down I went onto him again and this time he was with me, pulling at my hips so that he was in as I ground down.

He filled me. God, there were years of wild lovemaking ahead for him and any woman lucky enough to get near him. I pressed myself over him, let him bite and fondle, saw the blood rushing in his face as we started to jerk and rock together. I was really riding him, really wanted to hurt us both, wanted him to suck me while we did it, suck me so hard it would make me scream with pain, knowing my willing pupil would do whatever the hell I told him.

I was jacking up the rhythm, rocketing up and down his cock. I needed to ease the urge to come, but of course that only made it worse and more intense and I was getting tighter and tighter, holding him like a vice, and his cock was getting even harder with each frantic thrust, ramming right up inside.

'Tell me I'm the best you ever had,' he suddenly shouted, grabbing my hips and lifting me off him. 'Want to hear you say it.'

'Shut up and fuck me, big boy.'

His nails dug into me. 'Tell me, you bitch, tell me I'm the best.'

I stared at him. His cock was enormous now, so swollen, standing away from his flat stomach and aiming like a battering ram at my wet, waiting cunt.

'You're the best, baby,' I said. And I meant it. I'd never had someone so young, so gorgeous, so well hung, so strong, so eager, so fresh, so obedient, all in one package.

Then his cock slipped up inside again. I was trapping him inside me and going at him so that we were welded together, releasing him so that he could draw back, trapping again as he tensed his buttocks and thrust inside, throwing his head back, pulling my tits with his teeth, thrusting faster now and faster, hearing my own crackling gasps of pleasure as I came and he saw me coming and he laughed with disbelief as he tensed and hardened to bursting point and shot it up me.

I slumped forwards onto his chest and listened to the drumming of his heart. I thought my head was empty, but I heard myself say, 'I wish that was your first time. I wish I'd been the one to break you.'

His laugh rumbled under my ear. 'Make me, you mean.'

I went to sit on the chair opposite, my legs sluttishly apart. I started to do up the buttons of my blouse, just a couple of them.

'Wait till the boys hear about this.'

He sat up, pulled on his shorts, cracked his knuckles.

The boys. He was just a boy, here for the summer. For God's sake, what was I thinking?

'You're going to brag? Boast to them how you had the old dear from the B and B? Do you think they'll look at me different?'

He shrugged as only youngsters can. He went over to the mirror and raked his hair with his fingers.

'The old dear can take it!' he said. 'Respect! Think how the takings will go up when they hear how horny she is!'

'Do you think they'll want a piece of me, then?' I picked up my knickers, flicked them over his shoulder, round in front of his nose. I saw his long eyelashes curve down as he breathed in. 'Oh, I do hope so!'

He turned his head and looked at me. 'I was only joking, Sara – don't be pissed off.'

I kissed him, licking inside his mouth and very gently putting my hand on his dick. Not quite subsided. They can do it over and over, these randy lads.

'Do I look pissed off? Quite the reverse, honey.'

I tossed the knickers over a chair and pulled a silky dress over my head.

'I'd better go, then –'

'When they come back, honey, tell them they can come up here after hours.'

He stopped at the door. Oh, this was almost the best bit, because I knew it would happen. I knew there was going to be so much more of this. Such a baby, he couldn't tell if I was serious or not.

'If they want to have a laugh, I'll show them how. You know I can do that, don't you?'

I licked my finger, just as I did outside, held my dress open and rubbed my nipple. He bit his lips.

'I bet I can say it better than you can. Wouldn't they like to hear how you touched me, touched me right there in the garden, how you followed me up here, how you sucked my tits just like I wanted it?'

'Sounds pretty horny, doesn't it?' He swallowed hard.

I nodded, working my fingers, pinching my nipples as desire tore at me again. 'But how about, instead of telling them, you and I just show them? They can come up here, they're always welcome.'

'All of them?'

I started to stroke both breasts now, spreading my legs over the arm of the sofa. 'Sure. How I was on top, they can all come and watch how we did it, and then they can all take turns. I could have two latched on at a time, one on each tit –'

My pussy clenched furiously at that thought. It's doing it now as I'm telling you.

'– like puppies they can suck, and then you can fuck me, or they can do it, your mates, one by one, all together, from behind, underneath. Baby, I don't give a shit how they do it, so long as they can go on all night.'

He didn't need telling twice. He was right there, this time throwing me down on the sofa, scrabbling to get his cock out, pinning my arms over my head, biting at my breasts. He was the big man now.

Dear Fuckbook
Kyoko Church

October 15

I need a place to vent. This has to be it. I've never been a Dear Diary sort of person. To me it reeks of teenage angst. Oh, God, to be starting it at forty-three ... I am officially old and sad.

What to say? Where to start? They say, begin at the beginning. But I can't. Not right now. I haven't the strength. It would take too long, be too painful. I just need an outlet. So I'm going to start with a rant.

I fucking hate cell phones! Do people even call them cell phones anymore? God, I'm so out of touch I don't even know what to call them. Personal, hand-held, bloody instruments for ruining a marriage! Oh, God! No. It's too much. I can't do this.

November 1

Let's try again.

I'm not even going to go there this time. I'm going to start with the positive.

I went out last night! I mean, *out* out. The kind of out I used to go when I was twenty-one. Except that when I was twenty-one I didn't appreciate *out*. Not really. *Out* was just what we did on a Thursday – a Thursday! – or Friday and definitely on Saturday. Does twenty-one, single with no kids ever appreciate *out*? I certainly didn't. But I did last night!

I went out. And I hooked up. That's what they say now, right? That's what I'm saying. I fucking hooked up. And I say 'fucking' now too!

Let me tell you about the old me. The old me was a scared little girl. She did what she was told. She looked down when she walked. Never met anyone's eyes. Never got hit on. Never got laid.

I retired that scared, pathetic little girl last night.

I must say, I like the new girl. No matter how much pain was needed to birth her. Birthing hurts. That's a fact. This one was no different.

But now she's here. The new girl walks with her head up. She's got confidence. She meets people's eyes. And it's amazing the friends you make when you meet people's eyes.

I cannot understate how good it felt to walk into that club last night and not know what the end of the night would bring. There were possibilities. Possibilities! What a delightful word! Not casserole dinner and watching TV and no talking and perfunctory sex, no! Fuck that. Give me strangers and conversation and flirting. And sex. Sex that's anything but perfunctory.

Hold on, I'm getting ahead of myself! First: I looked HOT last night. Hot! Me! I've never looked hot in my life but here's something fabulous about a seriously less than fabulous situation: when your heart is broken you don't want to eat. So you lose weight! It's the diet secret of the century! I can just see the commercial:

The problem with other diets is that they don't deal with those pesky cravings. You're eating a salad but you're thinking about dill pickle chips. With the Heartbreak Diet those cravings are gone! Your stomach is constantly churning. Your head is wrapped in pain and trauma. Cravings vanish! Hunger, gone! The pounds melt away. Friends will be jealous and ask how you did it. Only you'll know the secret: The Heartbreak Diet! (Cheating Husband and Conniving Bitch Best Friend sold separately.)

A marketing possibility, I'd say. But I digress.

I took my skinny ass to the mall and bought the hottest, sluttiest outfit I could find. Black. Lots of skin. Lots of cleavage. I put on all the makeup my mother forbade me from wearing in junior high.

And.

I.

Went.

Out.

Oh, yes, there's a new sheriff in town.

She's fucking guys and not taking last names.

November 5

Tonight was Bradley.

I met Bradley last Thursday. Bradley is basically the guy in high school whom I wrote love letters to that I never sent. It's the age-old story: geeky bookworm secretly loves football jock. If only I wore black-rimmed glasses and had my best friend Alicia Silverstone give me a makeover, it could have been the fourth most popular John Hughes film of its time. In reality it was twenty-five years in the making. And my best friend was too busy with my husband's cock in her mouth.

The sheriff had her warpaint on. She was meeting stares. And returning them. Bradley was the third guy to buy me a drink and the first to pique my interest.

I say he was the jock from my high school but in fact he couldn't have gone to high school with me. Because when I was in high school he wasn't born yet.

There is something so delicious about the young ones, isn't there? And boom, just like that, I'm a cougar. Who knew? Not Bradley. He still thinks I'm twenty-six.

I'll admit, the lights were low. In the club, all the way home in the cab, back at his little apartment over the tattoo shop, the lighting was thankfully dim. Was it naughty of me to keep up the charade? When he saw the photo of my daughter on my phone and asked if it was my sister, what should I have said? I don't know now and I didn't know then, which is why I kept my mouth shut and the lights dim and half my clothes on while I straddled his condom-sheathed cock. He soon forgot.

Bradley with his thick thatch of dark hair, on top and below, his muscled and tanned young body, his smooth skin almost hairless, his dark eyes that have yet to be jaded by mortgages and early-morning feedings and lay-offs and … disappointment. Oh, he was so good, so trusting, so eager.

When he first said, 'Shit, babe. Why are you slowing down?' I admit I got off on that a tiny bit.

'Shhhh, Bradley, it's OK' is what I bent over and whispered in his ear as I stilled my naked body on top of him. 'You want this to be fun for me too, don't you? I haven't come yet.'

I wonder how many girls Bradley's fucked in his young life. I'm sure there have been quite a few, handsome as he is. I'm equally sure they were pretty one-sided romps on the pleasure scale, judging from the way he seemed so ready to just blow inside me as I rode him.

Here's another secret: I've always wanted to know, what's it like to make a guy wait?

What's it like to make a guy want it so bad he'd give you his car, sign over his last penny, curse his mother, sell his soul, just to be allowed release?

I wanted to experiment early on with the person whose name shall not be mentioned here, but he wasn't interested. Waiting made him impatient and annoyed. So I've only ever explored in my imagination. It's been my naughty secret for the last twenty-odd years. But now the gates of the playground of my imagination have been broken wide open. I cannot run out fast enough.

I wanted to make a guy wait. I wanted to feed off his desperation. What would happen if I did? I wanted to know.

And at that moment I decided Bradley was gonna help me find out.

November 6
Had to put you away last night. It was a late night already with my new little friend so by the time I got to you, Dear Diary, I could barely keep my eyes open.

But before I continue to tell you the tale of Bradley, let's change your name. I hate Dear Diary. Let's call you Dear Fuckbook. Because that's my dream for you.

What a night young Bradley had! What an eye-opening, cock-pulsing, desperate night of begging! Oh, it was delightful.

Once he realised he had to at least pretend to be a gentleman by giving me a chance to come first, he submitted to me slowing down. To me riding him in long, sensual glides up and down his pole. But pretty soon that was getting difficult for him too.

He grabbed my hips on a downthrust and stopped me. 'Uh, are you close yet?' he asked, puffing. Was it wrong of me to take pleasure in the innocence of that question. Of that look in his eyes?

I told him how I like to come by rubbing my clit down hard on the base of his cock, how I need to angle myself just so. It was so cute the way he asked me to go ahead and do that, then. He said, 'I can last, just not forever, you know.'

'Can you?' I asked. God, I'm naughty.

'Can I what?'

'Can you last?'

Apparently Bradley thinks of himself as quite the stud. He assured me he would be able to last. And really, I would be doing the guy a disservice not to test him on it.

So I pushed myself down on him. And oh, it was good. I was really horny by that point so that when my hard, swollen clit mashed down on the base of his cock it took only a few minutes of strong, rhythmic movement of my skewered pussy on his rock-hard dick before I burst into the first shuddering, pulsating orgasm of my new life.

And here's just a note about that orgasm. I mean, I guess there's no such thing as a bad orgasm, and certainly there was no lack of them in my old sex life. But this one. It had power. It had strength. I rode that cock hard, with intention, with complete focus on what felt good to me and me only.

And I came.

When I opened my eyes and remembered Bradley he was lying beneath me, panting, but with a look of amazement. Apparently he's never had a recently released cougar have one of the best orgasms of her life while riding his cock. Oh, there was so much pride in that look too, as if it was all him, smug little bastard.

'See? I told you I could last,' he said, all sweat and smiles.

'You did. But, aw, do I only get one?'

I know. I know it's really bad of me to think the look on his face in that moment was hilarious. But spank my ass and call me Mary because right there, on top of him with my pussy all relaxed from that huge orgasm and his cock all hard and needy and thrust up inside me, I laughed. I giggled so much just the movement almost sent him over so I had to jump off.

When I told him he could climb on top of me I could read the look in his eyes. That look showed confidence; he was thinking now he could call the shots and control the stroking. Did he notice the little twinkle in *my* eyes?

He positioned himself between my legs, put his condom-covered cock at my opening with his hand and eased himself in. Mm, it was nice. He started off at a good pace. But soon, of course, he picked up speed and started slamming it into me.

I stopped him. I twisted my body away from his cock so he couldn't push into it.

'Aw, dude!' (Dude. To me. A forty-three-year-old woman. This is how twenty-six-year-olds talk now, apparently. Even during sex.) 'No! Why are you stopping me? Are you ever gonna let me come?'

'Of course!' I giggled. 'It's just, you're doing it so hard! It hurts a bit.' It actually felt fucking amazing being rammed into at full speed. But Bradley didn't need to know that.

I told him, 'You can come. Just make sure you do it gently. Not so fast. Not so hard. You can do that, can't you?'

He assured me he could. With a voice deeper and gravelly with lust he said, 'Yeah, I can do it that way,' as he started thrusting again.

Alas, I must report, he could not. Or, at least, not as far as I was concerned. Because each time his orgasm loomed closer, his hips helplessly bucked forward, like a dog in heat, and just began jack-hammering into me. I must have stopped him ten times, and, oh, how each time he begged me not to. But stop I did, because, ooo,

I'm such a fragile little thing. He mustn't slam into me that way. Wink.

Finally I pushed him off me. I shushed his panicked protests and assured him he would get his much beleaguered orgasm. 'But,' I told him, 'you just have to do it the way I say. And it's apparent that you can't do it the way I want with my pussy. So now we'll try it with my mouth.'

Imagine wrenching an ice-cream cone from a small child. And then handing him a bag of chocolate-covered sunshine and candy-coated rainbows. Such was Bradley at that moment while I stood him up, knelt before him and peeled the condom off his hard prick.

His cock was uncut. And the head at this point was an angry shade of purple. 'Awww,' I whispered, as I grabbed the base of his shaft and pressed that sensitive flesh to my wet lips, pushed it into my hot mouth.

He bucked and shook and immediately started thrusting and calling out, 'Oh, God! Oh, God!' I couldn't have that. I pulled his cock out of my mouth and warned him again. I told him that, if he absolutely could not hold still, I would be forced to stop. And go home.

That made him focus.

Sitting here typing this, I still get all creamy when I think of the noises he made, the nonsensical words he spouted, the way his body shook so violently. I could tell just how hard it was for him to be still while I coaxed what was no doubt the most earth-shattering orgasm of young Bradley's life out of his cock with my mouth.

As he crested I had mercy on him. I took my mouth off and pumped his cock with my sloppy wet hand at a nice steady pace. Even though his hips thrust uncontrollably then, I kept going. I knew he really, physically could not stop that.

I couldn't help but be impressed with the volume of the jets of come that burst up out of him, the heights they reached, how long they lasted. I pumped and pumped and Bradley screamed out his relief, all 'yes' and 'God' and 'fuck' and 'Christ'. If his neighbours called the cops to register a noise complaint I would be unsurprised.

So that was Bradley, Dear Fuckbook.

Who will be next?

November 23

I dated a bit after university. I didn't marry right away. But I was always worried about seeming promiscuous. So I didn't sleep with many guys before I got married. Because that's what you did then, you got married. I had these old-fashioned notions about what a guy wanted in a girl he would marry, these sayings in my head, like about cows and milk and getting it for free. I thought of myself as a nice girl. I didn't want to be a slut.

Today I have no such concerns.

Such closed-minded thinking.

Who do I have to tell you about today, Dear Fuckbook? Well, actually there are a few. You see, I've been busy.

There was Arturo. He was lovely, if a little slow. Not such a great conversationalist was Arturo, but his massive cock more than made up for his smallish intellect. We fucked standing up in the alleyway outside a club.

Then Jason. Jason was the kind of guy who projected goth dom, what with his shit-kicking boots, his leather jacket, his shaved bald head, the piercings all the way up both ears. I could tell he was a teddy bear though. No amount of leather or piercings could mask the sweet sparkle in his soft blue eyes. We went back to his loft apartment and I used a strap-on in his ass to subdue him. I spanked him as I fucked his hole and precome dribbled down his erect shaft while he whispered for Mommy to stop, he'd be a good boy.

Vikram and Russell were next. They told me they'd been best friends since first grade, had shared everything, so naturally I asked them if they shared women too. They looked shocked. So uptight for thirty-somethings! But they're all the more open-minded, not to mention tight as friends, now that they've felt each other's prick through the thin membrane of skin between the pussy and ass of the woman they were fucking. Namely, me.

And finally Stephanie. I mean, I'm pretty hetero on the sliding scale of sexual orientation. But Stephanie's short, punky black hair and striking blue eyes just sparked something in me. She raised the act of licking pussy to an art form. God, to have that slithery creature's mouth on my quim! She used her tongue like a fine artist uses a brush, licked me in the most knowing way I've ever experienced. Plus, I learned a thing or two. You see, you think you're going to know how to do it, seeing as you have access to the same equipment and you know how you like it, but then you get down there and realise you have no fucking clue. But she was patient and willing to offer advice, as she panted and shook and pointed, no here, love, lick it right there, oh, God, yes, just like that. Lucky for Stephanie I am a quick study.

But here's another truth about something, Dear Fuckbook. As much as I'm having the sexual time of my life, quite literally a coming of age, there is an elusive something missing. I can't say what exactly. But, as I meet these delightful people and try these new things, I have a feeling that there is something even more just around the corner.

It's almost as though … someone is waiting for me.

December 12
The prophetic nature of that last entry scares me just a bit.

I am waiting here, Dear Fuckbook, to meet the most amazing man I have ever known.

Do I need to lay out the particulars? The chat room we met in, the interests we share, all the emails flying back and forth that led me to realise who I really am, the reason for neglecting you for these past three weeks? It doesn't matter.

All that matters is that in just about half an hour now the doorbell will ring. I will answer. And he will be here.

December 13
Dear Fuckbook, how I cannot wait to tell you what transpired.

I could bore you with all the details of my anticipation, of our slightly awkward initial greetings, of my first impressions of seeing the man of my dreams for the very first time and how he reminded me of Colin Firth, just a nice man, no hint of the twisted, horny leanings of the man he'd revealed to me over the past weeks. But you are a Fuckbook not a Romance book. So let's get to that.

He sat down on a chair.

'Come here, pet,' he said.

I was giggly. A giggly little forty-three-year-old school-girl. I felt ridiculous but I couldn't help it. His presence in my little house was so overwhelming. All the things we'd emailed about were all things that lived only in my fantasies. The words hadn't even been spoken aloud. And so to have this embodiment of my fantasies sitting on a chair in my kitchen seemed so completely unreal, like my world had shifted, tilted a bit to the left, everything askew and strange and therefore hilariously unbelievable.

In the best possible way. I never wanted real life to come back. A shaft of light broke into my kitchen, fell across his lap and shone so brightly at that moment. All I could do was grin like a madwoman, giggle uncontrollably.

'Now, puppy,' he said. 'Listen to me. We need to make you focus.' And he looked at his knee.

My heart dropped into my stomach.

I knew what he meant. We'd emailed about it. The fantasy of it drove me insane with lust, but, again, reality was so much different.

He sat closer to the edge of the chair so that half of his thigh extended from the edge of the seat with nothing underneath. 'Heel,' he said.

Oh, how I didn't want to at that moment. I really didn't want to. But, as I looked up from his knee to his eye, I suddenly walked forward with ease. I would do anything for the look of control in his eye. Anything not to disappoint him.

I straddled his knee. So close to him now. I could smell him, just faintly, this man whom I'd only ever seen in my dreams before today and couldn't even begin to imagine what he might smell like. Just hints of smells. Soap. Shampoo. Deodorant. And underneath, just barely, his own scent: woods and something musky. I wanted to bury my face in his neck and inhale. But that's not what he commanded. 'Heel,' he'd said. He nodded at me then and, even though his look was stern, his eyes shone.

I pressed my cunt down on his upper thigh.

'Good girl,' he said, low. 'There's my good little puppy. Now I know you want to do what all little puppies like. Go ahead. You know the rules. I know you'll stop when you need to.'

I grabbed the corners of the seat, behind his ass, and began to rhythmically ride his upper thigh. I laid my cheek against his chest so he couldn't look at my face, so I could press my shame into him and so I wouldn't have to acknowledge what was happening or how much it ignited a fire in me.

In moments I was gasping, shaking.

'Aw,' he said, putting his hand in my hair, on the back of my head, holding it gently to his chest. Oh, God, for him to be holding me that way! His gorgeous scent strong in my nose, my cunt firm on his thigh, him all around me. I hovered close, my climax loomed. 'Does that feel good, little puppy girl?' he whispered.

'Yes, Sir,' I breathed. Oh, it did feel so good. All of that delicious pressure from the soft but firm flesh of his thigh pressed against the wet centre of my need. Even through all our clothes that pressure and just the fact of him, his presence, his smell, his voice, his words. I needed to stop. I desperately needed to stop.

'It's OK, you can stand up now. I know when it's too much for my little girl,' he said. Confirming that he knows me, knows what's best.

Shaking, I rose.

'It's time for some puppy training,' he said. And oh, Dear FB, I don't mind telling you, I swooned a bit.

He reached into a bag and pulled out a leather dog collar attached to a fine metal chain.

My stomach proceeded to complete a gymnast's routine in the lower part of my body.

You might imagine that a collar for this purpose would be black, might have metal grommets or spikes around it. But no.

It was pink.

He saw the surprised look in my eyes. 'Well, I wanted something pretty, for my pretty little puppy,' he said.

And my heart bloomed into a state of pure love for him.

He stood and fastened my new collar around my neck. He gave a gentle tug and led me to the bedroom. Without hesitation he removed his clothes quickly and sat down on my bed with his back against the headboard, his legs stretched out in front of him. I could see he was already erect.

I felt a sharp tug on the collar and took a quick step forward.

'Can't take your eyes off my cock already, little slutty girl?' he said. 'You'll look when I say you can, pet, and not before, understand?'

I nodded my assent.

He had me strip for him. He pulled me close to the

side of the bed with the leash and watched as I took off each piece of clothing at his behest. I tried my best not to look down at his swollen prick but it's like my eyes were drawn there by some force beyond my power. Each time I looked it was bigger and each time earned me a quick smack on my ass, sometimes with his hand, sometimes with the leather handle of the leash.

He took out a condom. 'Now, pet,' he said. 'Do you think you can be a very good little girl and put this on my hard cock without too much stimulation?'

'Yes, Sir,' I said, taking the little square of foil from him.

You might think this odd, Dear Fuckbook. Most stories you read about doms have them fucking their subs for hours. My Sir is not like that.

And I love it.

I love how horny he is. It's like he's so masculine, he has so much testosterone, he cannot keep it at bay. I love how turned on by me he gets. I knew he was so turned on watching me strip that I would need to be careful just putting the condom on. I took this task seriously. He was trusting me to do it right.

'You may look at my cock now, little girl. And proceed.'

I climbed up onto the bed, knelt between his legs and opened the package. Carefully, I rolled the thin membrane down his thick shaft, being careful not to touch too much on any of the areas I knew were sensitive for him: that gorgeous-looking head, along the ridge of it, the frenulum. Oh, how I wanted to, though. Those parts and all the rest of him were just calling out for my tongue to swirl around and caress them. It would be so good.

When the condom was on he patted my head. 'Good girl,' he said and his voice was low and thick with lust. 'I know that required some restraint for such an eager little puppy. So here's what we're going to do. You're allowed to fuck me whichever way you'd like. Play with your bone and hide it in whichever hole you wish, little pet. But here are the rules: you cannot come. And you cannot make me come until I say I'm ready. It's all up to you.'

Oh fuck. Fuck! I thought this was the hottest thing I'd ever heard. I imagined myself impaled on his rod and trying to control myself, trying to stop myself from pounding up and down on him in the desperate attempt to quench the aching fire burning at my centre. I thought it was the hottest thing. Until he said what he said next.

'If you show me you have enough control of that slutty, wet little pussy to accomplish this, then I will reward you, little girl. I will reward you with my tongue. Succeed in not making me come until I say and you will get just what you've always dreamed of. My hot wet mouth slowly licking your pussy, teasing your clit, making you scream and beg and plead for release.'

I could have said so many things at that moment to

tell him how his precious words made me feel. If only my brain could form words. But as it turned out I didn't need to. My body showed us both what words could not express.

We both watched as one tear of clear girl goo slid down the inside of my thigh. My cheeks lit up in flames.

He reached out with his finger, slid it up my thigh to catch the drop and sucked it in his mouth. 'You taste delicious, my pet,' he said softly. 'As I knew you would. You may begin.'

Dear Fuckbook, how do I do this? How do I put into words the most amazing night of sex I've never even dared to dream of? It was more than sex. When I straddled him and slowly eased my sopping, dripping hole down onto his shaft he breathed out, 'Look at me, pet. I want you to look in my eyes so I can watch you as you struggle so hard not to explode.' He finished that sentence just as my throbbing clit made contact with his base and, oh, God, I could only hold it there for a second before I had to back off, rise up, the look in his eyes alone almost pushing me over. Could he do that? Could he even make me come with his eyes?

'Oh, pet,' he said. 'Your tight little snatch feels like heaven around my cock.' And I couldn't help it, it was like my cunt heard his words and clenched of its own accord. He smiled. 'Oo, did your little pussy hear me talking about her? That felt nice, pet. A little too nice.

Not much more of that or there won't be any pussy-licking for you.'

And on and on, like that. What do I mean when I say it was more than sex? I've had sex. This was unlike anything I've ever experienced. It was slow. It was considered. It was intentional. Every movement mattered. Every touch. Every look. We were locked together in our own universe, on our own plane of existence. Until he finally said the words I was waiting for.

'I am ready to come now, my pet,' he said, hushed and deliberate.

He ran his hands over my stomach, over my breasts, pinched my nipples a bit. Then he took my hands in his. We locked eyes and I rode him in smooth, steady strokes. I'm not sure but I have a feeling I peered into his soul as I used my cunt to drive the man of my dreams into his own world of bliss.

And when he said he was ready to go down and clean me up with his tongue he could see that lust was sending such strong tremors through my body it was hard to move. So he swept me up in his arms, laid me back on the bed and kissed all down my torso, whispering his sweet placations into my skin: *shh, you're doing such a good job, trying so hard, you're so beautiful, you're my good girl, you're a good puppy, nice pet.*

When he arrived at my pussy he made good on his promise. It felt like hours he was down there, Dear

Fuckbook, it honestly did. He spread my legs wide, held my lips open even wider, so I felt opened up, like there really could be nothing left to hide, I was all unlocked, there could be no more secrets.

There was no need for secrets with him.

He said, 'A little eager puppy needs training so she can learn how to sit patiently and wait for her Master's command. To come.' Then he bowed his head between my legs, and flicked and kissed and poked and prodded and meandered around with his tongue when all I wanted him to do was, please, please, have mercy on me, lick me hard, lick me fast so that this aching fire maybe quenched. Except I also wanted him to do nothing of the sort.

So, of course, he did do it then. He licked me hard and fast and, oh, I wasn't ready for it and, God, I was almost there and ... then he stopped. Then he did it slow. And firm. Slow, firm, methodical licks that had me rolling, spinning, reaching those amazing heights ... and then he stopped again.

I told him once, in an email, that I had always dreamed of being edged to orgasm slowly with a mouth on my pussy until I was nearly insane with lust.

One must be careful what one wishes for.

Finally, when my quaking thighs threatened to render me unconscious and my voice was hoarse from screaming, he looked up from between my thighs. 'You've been a very good girl, pet. You've accomplished all my tasks and you've endured all my training. You've exceeded my expectations.'

'Come, pet.'

Then he bent down.

And licked me until I did.

I'm with the Band
Elizabeth Coldwell

Nothing ever excited me like being in the heart of a packed rock club, part of the crowd that surged towards the stage, bodies pressed together in a hot, heaving crush, moving as one to the music. Looking up at the singer, or the guitarist, shirtless in the sex-charged atmosphere, and wanting him with a need so intense it left me panting for breath, and my underwear soaking wet. Knowing the night would come to a perfect end if only I could give myself to my idol backstage, letting him fuck me in all the delicious, exciting ways I'd so recently discovered.

Funny how I'd forgotten this, buried away that pent-up lust and desire before I'd ever got the chance to explore it properly, settling into the dull confines of marriage with John and abandoning all my rock-chick dreams. Yet it all came flooding back to me as I stepped inside the doors of the Sapphire Club, entering a world I thought I'd left behind me for good.

The place had hardly changed: still the same black-painted walls in the lobby, plastered with day-glo posters for forthcoming shows, and the same worn carpet, studded with cigarette burns, sticky beneath my boots. John would have died rather than set one well-shod foot in a place like this, but I found my heart beating just a little faster as I pushed open the heavy double doors that led through to the main body of the club.

The long, low-ceilinged space welcomed me like an old friend, returning after more than twenty years away. Without the vague cigarette fug that always used to hang over any decent-sized crowd, that acrid mix of nicotine and something more exotic, the place now smelled of sweat and bourbon, sharp enough to make me wrinkle my nose. When had I become quite so fastidious? And when, I wondered, reaching into my shoulder bag for the purse that lurked with the rest of my trinity of essentials – lip gloss and mobile phone – had I forgotten how many nights I'd spent standing by this same bar, hoping to catch the eye of some guy who might buy me the drink I couldn't quite afford on my wages as a temp? Since the divorce, I did everything on my own terms, paid my own way, and I enjoyed the feeling of independence, embracing it fully for perhaps the first time in my life.

I took another look round the club. Already, the crowd stood half a dozen deep in front of the stage, as people found the best vantage point for watching the acts on show. Where I stood, right by the bar, had always been the spot for those who judged themselves too cool to clap, more interested in drinking and schmoozing than in paying more than a cursory interest in whoever might be performing. With good reason, most of the time. If you played the Sapphire Club, you were either on the way up or the way down. Very few bands at the height of their power graced the Sapphire's stage, apart from the odd big name playing a warm-up show before embarking on a tour of major venues, or a secret Christmas gig for the benefit of the act's most loyal fans. Not that it had ever bothered me. All I'd cared about was the night out; a chance to have some fun and maybe meet a cute guy …

'What can I get you?' The barman, like almost everyone else in the room, appeared to be half my age, tattoos snaking down both forearms where they were revealed beneath his uniform T-shirt, black with the words SAPPHIRE CLUB over the left breast. He didn't blink an eye as I leaned in closer to answer his question, and my fears that I'd look out of place in such a young crowd faded just a little.

I'd been intending to ask for a glass of dry white wine. Instead, I found myself saying, 'Southern Comfort and lemonade, please.' Back in my clubbing days, I'd never drunk anything else, but, once I'd met John, I'd been educated in more sophisticated tastes. Now, taking a sip and relishing its sweet, familiar taste, I couldn't help but think of everything else I'd given up to fit in with John and his circle of friends. Over the course of twenty years, I'd become the dutiful corporate wife, dulling my own light to let my husband shine. And, once I'd become exactly what he wanted, he'd left me for his secretary, with her top-heavy tits and her willingness to give him blowjobs in his office when everyone else had gone home. How very predictable, how utterly John. Had anything good really come out of our marriage?

'Hey, Mum. You came.' The familiar voice at my ear startled me out of my maudlin thoughts. Correction. Had anything good come out of our marriage apart from Toby?

'Of course, darling. I told you I would.' I turned to give Toby a quick hug. His appearance in the club's annual 'battle of the bands' contest was the reason I'd come here tonight, and I suspected he was in need of a little reassurance.

'Wow, Mum. You look …' His voice tailed off as he took in my appearance, his expression one I couldn't quite read. When he'd invited me to the event, I knew I couldn't turn up in one of the boring black evening dresses I'd wear on a night out with John, or even my usual weekend wear of a little top and chunky cardigan over jeans. Instead, something had compelled me to go up into the attic and open a box of clothes I'd carefully stashed away once I was married, never dreaming I'd have any excuse to wear them again, but too sentimental to throw them away. So many memories were contained in that box, remnants of wild nights with good friends I'd somehow lost along the way, their lifestyle and mine no longer compatible – at least in my husband's eyes.

When I'd tried it on, the mock-snakeskin dress was a little shorter and rather tighter than I remembered, my tits and hips having filled out since I'd last worn it. The bumps of my suspender clips were visible beneath the stretchy fabric if you cared to look, but a club night had always demanded stockings, not tights, and I worked on the theory that the lighting in the Sapphire Club was always so dim you'd have really had to stare at my legs to notice – and, with so many young, hot girls in the crowd, who'd be staring at my legs? I'd teamed the dress with a denim jacket and ankle boots, and traded my usual diamond ear studs for dangling diamante. If the idea had been to turn myself into someone not even my son would recognise, it appeared to have worked.

'Can I get you a drink?' I asked.

He shook his head, indicating the bottle he clutched in his fist. 'I'm fine, thanks. They've laid on beers in the green room for all the bands taking part tonight.'

'Do you know where you are in the line-up?' I asked.

'Second. Probably the worst place we could be. They'll all have forgotten us by the time it comes to vote.' I turned at the sound of the new voice and saw Toby's best friend, Jack. He'd been the one who'd come up with the idea of forming the band, a couple of years ago, and, much to John's relief, it had been Jack's parents' garage they'd rehearsed in three or four nights a week. At last, their hard work had paid off, and Zombie Kill – and how John hated that name – had earned a much-coveted place in the battle of the bands.

Jack stared at me, too, but his expression was much clearer. Something very close to lust, as his gaze roamed the length of my nylon-clad legs, slowly working its way up my body.

'Hello, Jack,' I greeted him when he finally looked at my face. 'Nice to see you again.'

'Wow, you look amazing, Mrs Murdock.' The tone of awe in his voice almost made me laugh out loud.

'Call me Kay,' I requested. 'I've never been Mrs Murdock in this place.'

'You've been here before?'

'Oh, a long time ago now.' I decided against revealing too much of my past. Even if Jack had any interest in stories of the nights I'd spent here, and the men I'd gone home with, I didn't feel comfortable repeating any of them in front of my son. 'But I can tell you this was always the place to be seen.'

'Cool.' Jack's gaze slithered back down to my legs again, settling somewhere around the hemline of my dress.

Despite myself, I couldn't help looking at him as I might any man who'd shown signs of interest in me. Just past his twentieth birthday, he'd filled out in the last couple of years, growing into a frame that was close to six foot; taller and broader than Toby, though both boys shared the same artfully tousled hairstyle and scruffy stubble on their chin. He wore a short-sleeved plaid shirt, open to show his bare chest beneath it. A thin line of hair ran down from that covering his pecs, disappearing beneath the waistband of his jeans. How tempting it would be to follow that trail with fingers, or lips ...

I drew myself up short. This was Jack, my son's best friend; not at all who I should be fantasising over. Yet I couldn't stop thinking what he might look like, stripped of those jeans, cock hard and ready to be stroked.

'Hey, guys, give it up for Crimson Tide!' The voice of the DJ compering the night's event distracted us all. While we'd been talking, the first band on the bill had emerged on to the Sapphire Club's stage. A power chord rang out, accompanied by a blast of feedback, as they launched into a heavy, driving number.

'We'd better get back to the green room,' Jack said. 'The bands only get fifteen minutes, and we've got to be ready to go on stage pretty much as soon as they come off.'

'Well, good luck, darling. I'll be cheering for you.'

As Toby and Jack dashed off in the direction of the exit that would take them to the backstage area and the club's green room, I swore I heard Jack mutter, 'Your mum's turned into a real MILF, mate.'

Now there was an expression I'd never thought to hear in connection with my name. I knew what the acronym meant, of course, well aware that it was no longer considered shocking behaviour for an older woman to seek out a willing, horny young lover. And the thought that Jack considered me fuckable – it wasn't exactly the reaction I'd intended to arouse in him, but it made my pussy twitch with desire.

With difficulty, I drew my attention back to the band on stage. They really weren't my style – not now, not twenty years ago – with their doom-laden vocals and dramatic keyboard stabs, and, once I'd finished my drink, I took the opportunity to visit the ladies'.

As I stood looking into the mirrored wall behind the row of wash basins, applying another coat of wet-look lip gloss, two girls came into the room. One headed for an empty cubicle, while her friend stood outside waiting for her. That I'd forgotten, too; the ritual of visiting the ladies' in pairs, so you could bitch and gossip away from the bustle of the club.

'The band's crap,' the girl in the cubicle was saying, 'but I wouldn't mind giving the singer one. Did you see the size of his package?'

'Yeah,' her friend replied.

I hoped she wouldn't see my smirk reflected in the mirror; I'd discussed band members in similarly crude terms enough times in the past, speculating on what might be hiding in one pair of ultra-tight trousers or another. Though she probably didn't even notice me; if she saw me at all, it would only be as some old broad in a too-short dress, not someone who'd once shared the same ambitions she did, and dreamed of sleeping with the hottest guy in the band.

'Maybe we can get backstage, see if he's up for a fuck,' the first girl continued.

Even though I smiled at her enthusiasm, I knew I'd have a very different reaction if she'd been talking about Toby. Though I could have warned him about the lure of groupies till I was blue in the face, why else does any boy of that age dream of joining a band?

I wandered back out into the body of the club just in time to hear the DJ announce Zombie Kill. I pushed my way through the crowd and found a spot close to the wall, where I had a decent view of the band without being deafened by their speakers. When they were famous, I'd watch them from the envied spot in the wings, reserved for friends and family. Maybe I could have tried that tonight, pulling that old line, 'I'm with the band.' It wouldn't have been a lie.

But I liked the view I had. It gave me an uninterrupted

70

view of Jack, lost in his own world as his fingers shifted up and down the frets of his bass. The focus of the crowd was on Toby, who'd shed his T-shirt and whirled shirtless across the stage, and Chris, the guitarist, who it quickly became apparent was the real talent in the band, but I had eyes only for Jack.

They'd clearly connected with their audience in a way the previous act had failed to do. When they finished their fourth and final number, and took a bow, I yelled for more as loudly as anyone, even though they had to vacate the stage for the next contender. That proved to be a girl with an acoustic guitar, her voice pretty enough but her self-penned material a little too derivative for my liking.

Just as I was debating whether to get myself another drink, I felt a tap on my shoulder and turned to see Jack grinning at me. A thin film of sweat gleamed on his chest, and I fought the urge to lick it away.

'Hey, Mrs Mur– er – Kay. What did you think?'

'The crowd loved you. And I thought you were great. But what are you doing here?'

'Toby sent me out to find you. He thought you might want to come into the green room for a drink. He'd have come himself, but the guy who runs the club is talking to him about booking us again, whether or not we win the contest.'

'Really? That's great news. And yes, I'd love to join you all.'

I followed Jack out into the corridor, eager to go and congratulate Toby and the others for having made such a positive impression with the club owner, but we never made it as far as the green room. As soon as we were out of sight of anyone passing, Jack pressed me up against the wall, putting his lips to mine and kissing me hard. Even though I was startled by his boldness, I made no attempt to stop him, letting him push his tongue into my mouth and explore.

When he finally pulled back, he looked a little shame-faced, as if he couldn't quite believe what he'd had the audacity to do. 'I'm sorry if I've gone too far, but I just had to do that. I've been wanting to all night, ever since I saw those incredible legs of yours ...'

'Don't worry, Jack. I wanted it just as much as you did. And I wouldn't mind at all if you did it again.'

With that, I found myself in his arms once more, the kiss increasing in intensity as I twined my fingers in his dark hair and felt him grind his body against mine, the hard bulge in his jeans all too obvious. His mouth tasted of beer, his stubble prickled at my skin, and he kissed me with an eagerness John had never shown, not even in the earliest days of our relationship. I knew I shouldn't be doing this, not with someone who'd been a friend of my son since they were both at primary school, and whom I'd watched maturing from a lanky teenager into a finely built young man. I was much more experienced, and far too wise to throw myself at someone half my age. But that was what made it all so thrilling.

This time, when we broke apart we were both breathless, and my nipples pushed at the cups of my bra, tight peaks that almost demanded attention. Jack's eyes shone, his rising desire evident.

'God, Kay, I really need to fuck you.'

If I hesitated, it wasn't because of any reluctance on my part. I wanted Jack just as much as he wanted me. But we needed to find somewhere we weren't likely to be interrupted, and even in my clubbing prime I'd never been a fan of having sex in the toilets. Too cramped, too insanitary and downright inconsiderate of all the people who needed the cubicle you'd taken out of commission while you fucked.

Then it came to me. 'You said the manager's talking to Toby?' When he nodded, I continued, 'So that means his office is going to be empty. Let's go find it.'

The office was at the far end of the corridor, past the green room. From the half-open door came the sound of laughter and chatting, and I hoped no one glanced out and saw Jack and me passing by, rather than joining them as we were supposed to.

Jack tried the office door and found it unlocked. The room, when we slipped inside, was barely big enough to contain its selection of mismatched furniture: the club manager's desk, a battered filing cabinet and a squat black leather sofa whose cushions sagged with age. Signed photos hung on the wall, mostly of scantily clad female singers in provocative poses. Not exactly the working environment I'd want to spend my days in, but perfect for our immediate needs.

'Lock the door,' I told Jack. 'We don't want to be interrupted.'

He did as he was told, while I stripped off my jacket and dress. Jack stared open-mouthed at the sight of me in my lingerie and stockings. Whatever MILF fantasies he might entertain, it seemed clear I fulfilled every one of them.

'Strip,' I ordered him. 'Let me see that gorgeous cock of yours.'

I didn't usually issue demands when it came to sex, but it seemed I'd had a cougar lurking somewhere within me, just waiting for the right moment to be released. And, now I'd freed her, she wanted to be on top.

Jack dropped his shirt to the floor, then perched on the sofa arm to pull off his boots. Smiling at his eagerness to obey me, I slipped a hand under the waistband of my panties and stroked my clit while I watched him bare himself for me.

Socks and jeans discarded, he glanced at me before reaching to remove his briefs. Was he getting cold feet, worried that someone might notice he was still missing from the green room and wonder why it could be taking him so long to fetch me? Or was he simply distracted by the sight of my fingers moving beneath the thin pink panties, stoking my lust for him?

Taking a deep breath, he pulled down his underwear, cock unfurling to its full length. What a delicious thing it was. So hard, so strong – and able, at his age, to go all night.

But I was getting ahead of myself. For one thing, I'd forgotten to bring one vital item with me, never dreaming I'd need it.

'I don't have a condom,' I told him.

''SOK, I do. In my wallet.' He gestured to his discarded jeans. I found his wallet in the back pocket, flipped it open and extracted one of the condoms all young men seem to carry, usually more in hope than expectation. I ripped it open and rolled it into place, taking every opportunity to touch and tease his cock as I did.

I took off my panties, aware of Jack watching my every movement with rapt attention. The stockings I left on, knowing the suspender straps framed the one thing he wanted to see more than anything else, my pussy.

'You are so gorgeous …' he breathed.

'You're not so bad yourself,' I quipped, climbing on to the sofa and straddling his thighs. We kissed again, and I lowered myself just enough that the wet lips of my pussy brushed against Jack's cockhead. He groaned, jerking his hips up, needing more than just that brief contact. Reminding him who was in control, I pulled away, leaving him hanging. Only when he slumped back down did I ease his frustration, parting my lips with my fingers and guiding him into my hole.

It had been a while since I'd known the feeling of a thick hot cock surging into me – John had lost interest in fucking me well before the divorce – and at first I barely moved, just reacquainting myself with the feeling of being connected so intimately to another person.

Jack freed my tits from the cups of my bra and his mouth latched on to one hard nipple and sucked. Such a sweet sensation, making me arch my back with pleasure as Jack struggled to prevent the little bud slipping from his lips.

Only now did I begin to ride him in earnest, my pussy gliding up and down Jack's length in smooth, liquid movements. Somewhere, the battle of the bands continued, while Toby negotiated the first steps on the path to becoming a headlining act, but that might as well have been happening on a different planet. Jack and I were only concerned with each other, and the way our bodies fitted together, my pussy engulfing his cock, his mouth kissing a wet trail over my exposed tits.

Feeling the rise to orgasm begin, slower than I'd have liked, I dropped a hand between my legs, frigging my clit at the same time as I ground myself down on Jack's crotch. The sight caused him to stop suckling me, able to concentrate only on my fast-moving fingers.

'God, that's it,' he groaned. 'Make yourself come for me.'

His words of encouragement gave me the last push to send me tumbling into orgasm, pussy convulsing over and again around the thick shaft buried to the hilt inside me. My ecstatic cries echoed off the office walls, redoubled when I felt Jack shoot his spunk into the condom.

'We'd better get out of here,' Jack said, as he zipped himself back into his jeans. 'They'll be announcing the winner of the contest soon, and I've got no idea what the rest of the competition was like.'

'Believe me,' I told him, 'you've got no competition.'

I knew I should be regretting what I'd done – after all, I had no idea how Toby would react if he ever found out I'd fucked his best friend – but I didn't, not for a minute. Jack had managed to rekindle my love for rock bands, and the boys who played in them, and, now I'd discovered a lusty cougar lurked within me, I intended to let her loose whenever I got the opportunity. We let ourselves out of the office before we could be discovered, and went in search of the green room and a much-needed beer.

Katrina's Stallion
Kathleen Tudor

Katrina wasn't sure what it was about Cameron, but she couldn't seem to see him without feeling the blood rush through her body, sensitising her full breasts and causing a warm flush to settle low in her belly. Only problem was, Cameron was twenty-two, and her son's best friend.

The 'boys' came through the front door together, and, although her son hardly looked at her on his way through the kitchen, Cameron glanced up as always and gave her that sexy smile that set her arousal to a low simmer.

'Good afternoon, Mrs Moore,' he said, just like always.

'Katrina,' she said, her response automatic after more than two years of giving it. He gave his usual boyish grin in response, and she sighed as her son punched Cameron on the arm with an impatient 'Dude, come *on*.'

Now that he was here, they were sure to vanish into Jack's room and not emerge for a couple of hours, at least. She moved past his room as the explosions started, and into her bedroom, locking the door behind her.

What was it about this boy, really a man, if barely, who made her blood run so hot and her mind go blank except for images of him shirtless with that particular look in his eyes ... and, thanks to the pool in their back yard, she had an unseemly amount of detail on which to fixate when she imagined his defined, hairless pecs, his dusky-rose nipples and the curving definition of his abs.

She moaned and gave in, imagining how soft and warm his skin would feel as she ran her hands over his taut abs and down, following that dusting of hair down into his trunks to the warm, hot length of him ...

The explosions and sounds of gunfire from her son's gaming station were as loud as ever, and Katrina needed some relief if she was going to be able to concentrate for the rest of the day. She reached into the drawer on her side of the nightstand and found her vibrator, then set it on the pillow next to her and started a slow, sensual striptease.

Her fingers ran up under her shirt, tickling along her own ribs as she slowly peeled the fabric up and out of the way. She closed her eyes and lay back on the bed as she rolled her breasts in her hands, squeezing them and pinching her nipples until they were aching peaks of pleasure. Her fingers trembled as she reached behind her to unfasten the clasp of her bra, and the whisper of lace fell away as she returned her attention to her sensitive breasts.

She pushed all thoughts of appropriateness away and simply imagined Cameron standing over her, that adorable smile on his face and his eyes full of lust. She imagined him moving over her as he took her breasts in his hands and kneaded them gently, teasing and arousing her before he moved to slide her jeans down over her hips ...

The buzz of the zipper parting nearly made her moan aloud as she slid her hot hands under the fabric and pushed her jeans down along with her panties. She lay back, her body sensitive to the very air as she paused, savouring the moment of anticipation. She could practically feel his hands moving slowly over her body, starting at her ankles, and she clutched the sheet and tensed as if he were truly moving towards her centre.

Tentatively, she reached down to sample her own arousal and found herself wet and ready. She moaned as her fingers slid through the slippery wetness and found her clit, rubbing it gently in an erotic tease that made her pulse rush and pound in her ears and her breath come faster.

The vibrator hummed in the quiet room, cutting through the sound of the game in her son's room, and she thought of the real Cameron sitting there with a controller in his hand, oblivious to her fantasies about him only a few feet down the hall. The thought sent a fresh rush of arousal through her, and she touched the vibrator to her clit, unwilling to wait another second for satisfaction.

The powerful vibrations sent shocks of pleasure

through her on contact, and she pressed it against her clit, her hips bucking as she drove herself straight for the peak of pleasure. She bit her lip to stifle her aroused cries as she pushed herself higher and higher, then she closed her eyes and pictured Cameron again, this time grinning down at her as he poised to thrust his cock deep inside her. She gasped at the vivid image, and, when she imagined him plunging into her, her entire body clenched as the pleasure grabbed hold and shook her like an earthquake.

Katrina turned the vibrator off and lay still for several minutes, waiting for her breathing to return to normal. She savoured the prickles across her flushed body where beads of sweat had formed, and shivered whenever the scent of her arousal drifted up to her. Gradually her heartbeat and her breathing slowed, and she sighed as she shook the last of the languor out of her limbs and sat up.

Forget the age difference, Cameron was legal and he made every nerve in her body sizzle. She was quickly forgetting any of the reasons that she shouldn't pursue him if he was what she wanted. Even as she pulled her clothes back on and made sure her appearance was in order, Katrina was beginning to form a plan. Jack always left his phone out on the counter. Perhaps she should have 'Jack' invite Cameron over for lunch soon.

* * *

Katrina nearly shook with nerves as she waited for the doorbell to ring. She'd prepared a couple of turkey sandwiches and put them through her panini press, set out a small selection of snacks and made iced tea – she was quickly running out of ways to distract herself.

She'd just reapplied her lipstick and then wiped it off again for the third time when she finally heard the knock at the front door. Cameron smiled when he saw her.

'Hey, Mrs Moore.'

She didn't step back out of the doorway. Somehow the familiarity of his greeting broke through her nerves, and she leaned against the jamb, the door still too close against her side for him to pass. 'I'm not opening this door until you call me by my given name,' she said, her voice pitched seductively low, but light enough to be teasing.

Something in Cameron's face changed, and his eyes flickered down to take in the flirty knee-length dress she was wearing. 'Is Jack home?' he asked.

'No, he's in classes all afternoon,' she replied. She thought she did a credible job of keeping guilt from creeping into her voice.

Cameron stepped forward, almost as if he were going to push through the door, and paused so close that she had to look up to maintain eye contact. He was easily inside her personal space, and her body yearned towards him as if he carried some static charge. His voice was

82

pitched low when he replied, 'Then I guess I'm here to see you, Katrina.'

'I guess you are,' she said. Her voice was breathy, having lost that seductive depth, but Cameron reacted as if she'd reached out and stroked him. A shudder rippled through his entire body and he blinked hard. She let the door go, and he stepped past her so closely that his body brushed her arm as he came inside.

'I've got lunch ready,' she said, taking the lead again and guiding him to the table. He smiled as if he were trying to restrain laughter, and Katrina turned her back on him to hide her blush, hoping she hadn't misread what had just happened.

Cameron sat down at the dining-room table and helped himself to a handful of chips as she went into the kitchen to fetch the sandwiches and a couple of glasses of tea. She used the familiar routine of setting out food to nudge her back into control of herself and – she hoped – the situation.

For a few minutes they ate in silence, and a combination of frustrated lust and nerves danced through Katrina's stomach until she knew that she either had to do something now or lose her nerve completely. She raised one bare foot under the table, her eyes on her plate as she slowly reached out for Cameron. When she found his leg, her foot caressed his calf before moving up towards the outside of his knee.

Cameron sat up straight as if electrified, staring at her as he finished chewing his food and swallowed, hard. Then he smiled, and Katrina had the exciting sensation of being admired by a stallion. He shifted in his seat and Katrina looked up, locking eyes with him as her foot skimmed over his knee. He took another bite and chewed slowly, not letting up on the eye contact, and spread his legs to the edges of his seat.

Katrina lifted an olive to her lips and sucked it into her mouth as she took his invitation, letting her foot drift to the inside of his thigh and up towards his lap. When she encountered the hot, hard erection pressing back at her, the nerves finally vanished and she found that she could take another bite without a problem, watching him through her lashes as she caressed his stiff organ with her toes.

Cameron, on the other hand, was having trouble concentrating on his food. Katrina smiled as he put his sandwich down and clenched his teeth, biting off a moan. 'You do this to me all the time,' he said.

'If you mean footsie under the table, then there may be something Jack's not telling us,' she replied lightly, skimming up and down the length of him.

He reached into his lap and grabbed her foot, pressing it hard against his erection. 'I don't mean your foot, Katrina. I mean this.'

Tingles shot up and down her spine, but Katrina ignored them, opening her mouth and laying another olive on her tongue. She chewed thoughtfully before she replied, 'I never knew. If I had, I might have done something like this much sooner.'

'What about your husband?' Cameron released her and picked up his sandwich, and Katrina felt a wave of warmth for the horny young man making an effort to do the right thing.

'We discovered very early on that we're not sexually compatible. He wants more kink than I can give him, and I want more … staying power. We have an arrangement.'

'Then why are we still sitting at the table pretending to be polite?' he asked.

Katrina smiled. 'Come kiss me.'

He obliged, standing then moving around the table with the grace of the young and athletic. He reached for her and tipped her head back, holding eye contact with her for a long moment before he reached up with his other hand, traced a line up her throat that sent shivers through her body, and pressed his lips to hers.

His tentative kiss intensified quickly as he gained confidence, and Katrina let her tongue play out, teasing over his lips until he plunged his tongue into her mouth in an erotic tangle of taste and sensation. She licked the salt of the chips from his lips, and he moaned into the kiss as he explored every corner of her mouth. She felt as if she were floating, his hands locking her head gently in place as he kissed her so thoroughly her toes curled.

Then he moved, pulling her so softly upward that she practically floated out of her chair, coming to stand before him and letting her body press against his. His cock throbbed hard against her belly, and she whimpered as she felt the eager length of it, hoping that his youthful potency would come with the stamina to satisfy.

She tried to busy her hands on his back and in his hair, running across his skin, dragging through his sweet brown waves and teasing back down his face with soft strokes. Finally she couldn't resist her true temptation anymore, and her fingers moved down his chest in a slow tease towards her ultimate goal, spiralling and shifting into playful patterns, but moving ever downwards. When she reached his waist, she lifted one hand and plunged her tongue deep into his mouth as she grabbed his cock firmly for the first time.

Cameron moaned and thrust back against her hand, inviting her to the very places she'd fantasised about for months. Then he shifted, and she gasped in surprise as he lifted her off her feet. He grinned down at her as their kiss broke, and she liked the way that grin looked with the lust in his eyes.

He didn't carry her far, but set her down on the table and examined her up and down like she was a slice of German chocolate cake and he was only deciding where to take the first taste. She reached around for her zipper, opening the dress enough to allow the straps to fall away from her arms and reveal the turquoise satin of her bra. Cameron took the invitation. He lifted both of her breasts and weighed them in his hands as he teased and manipulated them with his fingers.

'I like it hard,' she said. 'Squeeze them. Pinch my nipples.' She had barely gotten out the last couple of words when he gave them a rough squeeze and released them, leaving her gasping and dizzy with desire. He reached around behind her and she felt the release of her bra clasp. Then he was pulling the bra away and tossing it behind him, into the kitchen.

She felt something cold on her nipple and the surprise made her whimper. Cameron held up a cold olive that he must have plucked from a dish, and held it to her lips, watching as she sucked it into her mouth. She moved forward and caught one of his fingers, sucking that into her mouth, too, and teasing her tongue around it as she hoped to do with his more sensitive appendage. He responded beautifully, and she watched his eyes flash a darker shade of blue as he moaned and gently fucked her mouth with his finger.

He pulled away, then, and trailed his finger from the corner of her mouth downwards, following its path with a searing line of hot kisses at the corner of her mouth, her neck, her collarbone and onwards. She prayed that he would find her nipple quickly, but he teased around it, kissing slow circles around it and making her moan and thrust her breasts towards his face.

'Damn it, Cameron,' she started, grabbing his head. But what was meant to be a commanding touch turned into a desperate grasp as his mouth finally came down over her nipple and she fisted her hands in his hair, holding on for dear life while his lips and teeth provided him with a direct line to her clit.

She couldn't – had never – but there was that building sensation, like a lit fuse that burned in anticipation, concentrated dually at her clit and on her breast, where he nipped gently and sucked hard, teasing with his tongue and lips. One hand released his hair and she started to reach for her clit, knowing that if she could just touch it she would be an instant from release. But Cameron bit down on her nipple, and a surge of pleasure and pain washed through her with convulsive force before she even got close.

She screamed as the orgasm exploded through her pelvis and breasts, meeting in the middle and washing back until her entire body was rocked with pleasure. Her breath stole away in the midst of the excitement and she panted for air, only then realising that she'd wrapped her legs around Cameron and had one fist buried in his hair, pressing his face so hard against her breast that he was probably having trouble breathing, too.

And even still, the cocky bastard was gently stroking his tongue over her nipple, plucking her nerves like a master harpist and drawing out the quivering pleasure from her bones. She released him and fell back, panting, and he stood over her, young and sure.

'That was cool,' he said, and he grinned that boyish grin again that made her insides melt and her pussy hotter than ever. She sighed as she looked up at him, and she realised how she must look, dishevelled from her orgasm, her dress pulled down to her waist, hair a mess, skirt in disarray, reclining across the dining-room table. She imagined that she looked like some sort of sexual feast, and she intended to entice this hungry young stallion to dine.

'Not a bad start,' she said, and leaned back on one elbow to draw the attention even further to her other hand, which had danced up the tent of her skirt and was now bunching the fabric, lifting it to reveal her feminine glory, all waxed and ready for Cameron with no panties to interrupt their pleasure. 'Are you ready for your dessert?'

Cameron hesitated, and she watched him lift one hand to stroke his heavy cock through his pants. She hoped he was trying to preserve this vision for the future. She liked the idea of him lying in bed, hopelessly aroused by the picture of her swollen cunt all exposed for him as he stroked himself.

He closed his eyes and a shudder passed visibly through his body, then he moved forward with slow, deliberate intensity and, with one last glance up at her from between her legs, slid his tongue deep into her slit.

Katrina closed her own eyes and let her head fall back, moaning as he ate her out, gaining both speed and confidence as the sounds of her pleasure filled the room and her hips rocked up to meet his mouth. She whimpered with aroused frustration, desperate to feel his hot mouth close over her clit, but she didn't know if his teasing was intentional or ignorance, and she didn't want to spoil it for him so soon.

He soon proved that it wasn't ignorance guiding his tongue. He lifted one hand and brushed his fingers gently against her clit, not enough to bring her to orgasm, but plenty to bring torturous sheets of fiery arousal through her body. She threw back her head and moaned wildly, but he maintained the tease for another minute, and she could swear she could feel him smiling against her cunt.

Then his fingers shifted to a firmer rhythm, and she could have sobbed with relief. A moment later his fingers were replaced with the hot mouth she really craved, and Katrina shouted in pleasure as he worked his magic, 'So close! Oh, Cam, just like that! So –' She broke off with a scream, and her hips convulsed up into his mouth as she rode the orgasm, a second's relief skimming through her before she felt the desire for *more*.

'I wish I'd brought the condoms out here,' she panted,' I want you to fuck me right here on the table.' She started to sit up, but Cameron blushed, of all things, and reached into his pocket.

'I have one,' he said.

She smiled a wicked grin up at him and leaned back, edging herself closer to the lip of the table. 'Oh, Cameron, you *are* my favourite.'

He unfastened his pants and she watched in breathless anticipation, teasing both of them by reaching between her own legs and stroking the wet, swollen flesh there. She was gushing with the fluid of her arousal, as horny as she had ever been. She felt another waveflood from her body and over her fingers when Cameron pulled his underwear away and stood, revealing his hard cock.

He was truly a stallion, built long and thick as though made just to fill her up, and Katrina prayed that he'd have the energy of a young stallion, too. This was what she'd always needed – what her husband could never provide – someone to fuck her over and over until she was exhausted, her needs finally sated and her prolific desire banked.

He noted her hungry gaze on his cock and smiled. 'My last girlfriend was afraid.'

'Come and see how scared I am,' she replied, widening her spread legs for emphasis. 'Look at me, I'm trembling.' She was; her desire had diffused through her every cell, and her entire body trembled in the quest for another orgasm – for further satisfaction.

Cameron rolled the condom on, then gave her a lewd look and rubbed his hand through her slickness, using it to lubricate his cock. He leaned over her slowly, and Katrina grabbed his upper arms, digging in with her nails. 'Fuck me, Cameron. God damn it, put that thing inside me and fuck me until I scream.'

With one hard thrust, he did, driving himself inside her in one smooth stroke. She arched up to meet him, her hips rising and her legs moving to capture his waist as she took every inch of him into her body, feeling pleased and full and yet still so hungry for more. She wriggled against him, and he pulled back and slammed his cock into her, forming a pistoning rhythm that she met, beat for beat.

Every fantasy she'd ever had about him came back to her as he fucked her hard on her dining-room table, and Katrina felt the pleasure begin to mount in her again as she took him hungrily. 'I'm going to come all over your cock, Cameron,' she cried, and inarticulate sounds of pleasure followed her declaration as she felt herself tip over the edge, spasming around his erection and squeezing him with her inner walls even as she tightened her arms and legs around him.

He continued to drive into her, and her heart could have burst at the joy she got from being fucked right through her orgasm, then, as it welled up and spilled out from her core, a second. 'Holy shit,' he whispered into her ear, and she screamed as she rode him hard, bucking up to meet his thrusting hips even as pleasure washed through her in what felt like a never-ending wave. 'Holy shit, holy shit …'

When her cunt clenched and spasmed around him for a third time, Cameron roared and increased his pace, pounding her into the table and digging his hands into her shoulders with bruising strength. He thrust one last time, deep inside her, and his entire body shuddered and then went limp. She panted as she stroked his hair and back and wondered if she should feel more dirty or wrong for fucking her son's best friend on the dining-room table in the middle of the day. Instead, she just felt excited, aroused and pleased.

Cameron climbed off of her, removed the condom, tied a neat little knot and folded it into a tissue that he slipped into his pocket. 'That was amazing,' he said.

Katrina slid off of the table and moved towards him with the liquid grace that she gained from sex and arousal. She stood on her tiptoes to place a kiss on his neck, just under his jaw, and reached down with her other to stroke his half-hard cock. He shuddered under her lips and his cock twitched against her hand as she slowly drew him back to arousal.

'What? Don't tell me you're finished. And I had such high hopes for you,' she murmured, nibbling at his ear. Cameron moaned loudly, and his cock pulsed again, tapping against her thigh as it rose. 'Good. Then come on, my dear stallion, the rest of the condoms are in my room.' She had about three more hours before she had to be concerned about anyone coming home, and she planned to get a lot of use out of that time.

A Wonderful Time
Olivia London

Delta May Crane looked in the mirror that morning for a fraction longer than she usually did. She wasn't being vain. She just wanted to know who she was supposed to be that day. She was a busy woman with friends and relatives who depended on her generosity and keen business sense. An employer, caregiver and doting auntie to a lovely niece who was her child substitute. Weeks could go by without Ms Crane giving a thought to herself and, as a woman who preferred giving to receiving, this seemed a normal state of affairs.

On this particular morning, the owner of Crane's Crumpets and Tea in Seattle's Lower Queen Anne neighbourhood was supposed to be a woman comfortable with her age. All around her, she witnessed middle-aged women experiencing midlife meltdowns. A science teacher in Delta's Wednesday-night book group mused aloud that lottery winners aren't the only people who go broke after a windfall. The instructor confessed to having inherited $100,000, only to blow the whole wad on analysis. She was broke in a year but thrice weekly she got to recline on a balding psychiatrist's Naugahyde couch and calibrate the envy of friends as she imagined her life becoming iconic, like a *New Yorker* cartoon.

Delta nodded in sympathy but, really, she had little patience with those whose climacteric challenges took the form of profligate spending. She had no rich uncle or patron saint smoothing the way to success. When she started her shop she had to make her crumpets using tuna cans with the tops and bottoms removed; it would require two years of fiscal responsibility before she could afford the stainless-steel pans she'd lovingly purchase from gourmet culinary catalogues.

Satisfied with her work, Delta tried to sublimate her desires by doing for others, and of course renting the occasional sexy French film.

She was through with dating. Delta had a knack for attracting what she called 'low-resolution' men for, after the fact of these men had dissipated, the details of them were rarely clear. She once dated a man who, when neither of them felt like cooking, would dine only at Thai restaurants. He'd order the spiciest items on the menu but push them away for being too explicitly hot. Then he'd pick at her dinner. When, exasperated, she asked him why he didn't order milder food he'd take offence, walk out and leave her with the bill.

No, dating was old news and Delta was more concerned with the fine print, the smalltype that read: *Lady, you need to get laid.*

Sometimes, Delta's superstitions made her feel old. Drop a knife – or was it a fork? – and, lo and behold, a man will walk into your life. Of course, the utensil had to be dropped by accident and preferably on a hard surface such as concrete or, in a pinch, linoleum.

Just thinking the words 'hard surface' drew her breath up short.

The morning of the day she decided to treat herself to a casual encounter, she had dropped a knife in the kitchen. An auspicious sign.

She knew her friends and colleagues would disapprove of answering 'Just Sex' ads on a casual dating web site, but that channel seemed safer than going to a bar. She would meet the guys for coffee first then, if chemistry ensued, the strangers in lust could go from there.

But there was never any lust. The guys didn't look like their pictures, or maybe they did but the flesh-and-blood versions gave off creepy vibes better left at the door.

She was about to give up when a handsome black-haired lad took a seat next to her at a café downtown, far enough away from Crane's Crumpets to set up an anonymous assignation.

'You look exactly like your picture!' Delta exclaimed, not wanting to add, 'Only younger.'

Her date's name was Conor and he was carrying a pile of books with him.

'Reading material in case you get bored?'

Conor laughed. 'Just got out of class. I'm in grad school.'

A student. Delta thought: I'm going to fuck a student. She suddenly thought of Mary Kay Letourneau, the teacher who made the headlines because she had a sexual relationship with a thirteen-year-old pupil, but that was ridiculous; Conor said he was twenty-six.

'You are twenty-six, aren't you?'

The young man gave her a reassuring smile. 'That I am. And you're the sexiest woman I've ever seen in my life.'

Delta blushed to the roots of her natural (albeit slightly encouraged) blonde hair. She had fretted over what to wear for this meeting. Too mature for a Betsey Johnson dress but determined to stave off muumuus for the dotage days, Delta May chose a nearly diaphanous silk blouse and form-fitting grey skirt.

Her voice was husky from the mountains of cigarettes she smoked in her first youth when many females of her generation believed the only way to a svelte figure was through a carton of Marlboro Lights. She hoped she sounded to him like a sultry cabaret singer and not a prison matron.

An Erotica Collection

They talked until it was time to order refills. Talked circles round the reason why they were really there until Conor flattened his palm under the hem of the horny blonde's skirt.

She could have jumped him right there. His fingers moved incrementally towards her crotch just for a tease of sensation and then his hands were gone and his fingers steepling over his ceramic mug.

The young know when they're in control but, if an eager fellow wants to get some action, he knows when to stop teasing and get serious.

'*Delta*,' he said, and just the way he murmured her name was like being given a chance to lick frosting from a spoon.

He leaned close enough so she could feel the intensity of him, the weight of his desire hammered with every breath. 'How badly do you want to go down on me right now?'

From another man this question would have been cause for alarm. She looked at him. He had a face she would summon in a dream. His hair thick and black and skin pale from the great indoors. She was conscious of an unremitting hunger and wanted only to sup on this perfect paradigm of maleness.

As if from a great distance, she heard herself say, 'I wouldn't mind.'

They hailed a cab to Conor's apartment on Capitol

99

Hill. Even on the way to getting his manhood sucked to oblivion, the handsome Irish lad expounded on the specialness of his brick building dating from the 1920s, the apartments soundproofed with double interior walls, hint, hint.

'You planning on playing a trumpet while I go down on you?'

'No, just, you know, in case we want to move on to other things.'

Delta arched her brow and smiled; she hoped she wouldn't have to remind him this was a one-time-only thing.

Conor went to the kitchen to search the cupboards for something cordial to offer his guest but she stopped him in his tracks.

'I don't need anything to drink,' she said. 'I just need you.'

She unzipped his tweeds and caressed his cock with her hands.

'I hope this doesn't interfere with your homework,' she couldn't resist saying as she kicked off her skirt and led him to the nearest horizontal surface.

She straddled him and kissed his entire face, lingering at his sweet sensual lips. She kissed his neck and collarbone, bussed him all the way down his chest until she was a pillow covering his groin.

She felt weightless and ageless at once. She was a

vamp and a co-ed, a vulpine vixen masquerading as the girl next door.

Delta let her tongue tickle the glabrous head of his cock before setting it loose like a pinwheel, her gloss aswirl, constantly in motion while her lips paid homage with tender care. It was as if her tongue was gloating, finally able to strut its stuff after a dearth of appreciation.

And she could tell her lover was appreciating such lavish attention by the way he ran his elegant fingers over her scalp, pausing to caress her temples even as she inhaled with the fullest measure of deep throat.

His cock throbbed and bobbed with the urgency Delta brought to her palate and when he came on her chest it was with a thunderous clap of glee.

He was so handsome, so inordinately good-looking that she wanted to run from this beacon of hope, lest she get caught up in something too fragile and beautiful to hold.

She stayed for dinner. Conor offered to make omelettes or stir-fry but Delta took one look at his platoon of non-stick fry tubs and suggested take-out or delivery. How she longed to replace the scarred culinary combat ware with Le Creuset saucepans! This is why she could never get serious about someone so much younger; there'd be too much temptation to do a makeover and then of course the one being Eliza Doolittled would start walking a fine line of resentment until that line became no thicker than a razor's edge.

No, this was just for fun. Just this once, Delta was determined to think about her own pleasure, not the needs of her employees, customers, vendors or relatives. Tonight was all about satisfaction without expectations.

They perused some take-out menus, finally settling on a large, overpriced gourmet pizza.

'Pizza!' Delta said with a laugh. 'I haven't ordered pizza in ages. Just promise you won't light a clove cigarette afterwards. And no smoking a doobie or we won't be satisfied with one pizza. People either don't see the cost-prohibitive side of smoking pot or they're too stoned to care. If you grow marijuana plants in your spare time, I don't want to know.'

Conor fossicked around a byzantine wine rack until he found just what he was looking for. When he held up a bottle of Pinot Noir for her approval, she nodded, duly impressed.

'You don't take me seriously because I'm a twenty-something grad student.'

Delta thought: I don't take you seriously because you placed an ad in a casual sex pickup column. This wasn't supposed to be serious! Still, she knew what it was like to be objectified (she was young once herself) and didn't want to make anyone feel bad. This adventure still had a lot of feel-good potential.

'Conor, you're obviously serious about your studies. I admire that. It's just, well … the way we met.'

'People meet – and find love – in the most unusual places these days.'

Love? Was he kidding? 'Conor, I'm old enough to be your –'

Cutting her off while deftly handing over a glass of wine, he said, 'Unless you started menstruating at eleven or twelve, you are not old enough to be my mother.'

'I'm old enough to be your doting auntie,' Delta reasoned, crossing her arms over her chest. 'I could have bought you your first baseball glove.'

'Let's change the subject,' Conor said, which was easy to do because just then the pizza arrived with all its garlicky distraction.

After they had fed each other slices and finished another bottle of wine, Delta realised she wanted to go down on this perfect specimen of maleness again.

'Are you serious?' he asked, tracing her lips with his thumb.

'I am seriously enjoying myself with a serious young man and, yes, I seriously want to go down on you. If you're assigned an essay for this assignation, you can call it "Blow Job Redux".'

Conor pulled her to his chest for a long, sweet kiss, deep and joyful. Before he could lose sight of her mission, Delta was all over his cock again, sucking with a vim that could have pulled a fitted sheet off a bed and turned it into a scrunchie.

She was down on her shins stroking his cock with every persuasion of her tongue, drawing a velvet curtain round the base of the shaft, when he lifted her up and took her by the hand, took her to the bedroom.

They started out with her on all fours, no need for foreplay; she had been a steady stream of surrender from the moment Conor asked her how badly she wanted to go down on him.

With his hands commandeering her hips, Conor leveraged his cock until he was halfway in, enjoying a moment of exquisite control even as Delta reached back to squeeze his hamstrings, propel him forward.

Slippery as she was, she was tight too; he had the sensation of a silk cord tying a knot round his member and he had to quickly think of something sobering. He imagined himself forced to live in a yurt or, no, better yet, an igloo, lest he explode before the rapture even began.

Finally, he pushed and pumped his way to her most vital core as she beckoned his cock to a place of submission so sweet and so uninhibited he felt exalted at the point of orgasm rather than drained. There would be no tristesse with this giving, sensual female. He would live for the moment when he could fill her vulva again, fill it with his love.

A few beads of sweat had gathered at the small of her back and he kissed those away before encouraging her into a supine position.

They spooned and murmured endearments in their post-coital bliss. When Conor began to caress Delta's breasts and belly, she was liquid again, her loins sleek with desire.

'Touch me,' she whispered.

He touched her, awed by her want. He penetrated her snuggery with agile fingers, pumping her mound and engulfing her clit, bringing her to orgasm that way over and over.

Eventually, she came so hard she was trembling and that's when he mounted her in the missionary position, drew her legs up into a vigorous V and pinned her to the counterpane with the sure deep thrusts of his cock. He looked into her eyes and kissed her brow and told her how much he needed her.

She needed this possession, this singular act of carnal devotion, but she didn't dare allow herself to think beyond the moment. She twined her arms round Conor's neck and they rocked each other into riotous joyful fruition.

After love, they took a long, hot shower together and fell back into bed. She loved the way he smelled before and during sex; now she breathed in the fresh, clean scent of his youth. A sensitive youngish male with his whole life ahead of him. How many pretty co-eds were dreaming of Conor right now?

He must have assumed she was spending the night for

he mentioned a new coffee shop on Broadway where they could breakfast together in the morning.

She had no intention of spending the night. This was just 'a bit of *craic*' as Moira, an energetic and lovely Irishwoman in her reading group, would call it, *craic* (pronounced 'crack') being Gaelic for merriment. Yes, she and Conor had had a merry time but there was nothing but folly in dating a younger man. Delta blinked away the memory of her Grandma Lil. Lillian Crane was active well into her nineties with a boyfriend thirty years her junior. She drove a marshmallow-white Cadillac, combed her hair up into a beehive and listened to rock music. Delta always smiled thinking of her gran: the original cougar.

But Lil was what everyone in the family called 'a character' and Delta was cut from a different cloth, cheesecloth perhaps, given the voluptuous blonde's love of all things culinary. Delta couldn't remember a time when she didn't have to weigh every decision with its sobering outcome. She paid her dues in the food service hierarchy and that alone was reason to be grateful for the respect she now enjoyed as a mature, successful businesswoman. She didn't 'marry up' to get where she was and never accepted favours she couldn't pay back with the luscious fruits of her own labour. She got where she was the old-fashioned way: she baked and cooked for it.

It still gave her indigestion to recall the more humbling

moments of those early catering days. She had often heard people from other professions bemoan their 'salad days' but cooking professionals must survive the spanakopita and chicken satay circuit.

Delta had a catering gig the week after her thirtieth birthday. One of the bridesmaids asked her if maybe she wasn't a little too old to be serving *hors d'oeuvres*.

'I'm not old,' the caterer intoned.

'What I mean to say is: you're attractive. You should try to marry before it's too late for you.'

Delta kept her mouth shut. There is no adequate rejoinder to those who employ your services; a sharp-tongued '*touché*' or barbed comeback will typically lose you your job.

Six months later she took out a small business loan and started her crumpet shop, which also did outside catering. She had a reputation for being a fair and generous employer. If an employee turned thirty or hit any other milestone on her watch, he or she received a paid day off and a picnic basket filled with food and wine.

Delta yawned. After all that delicious sex and Pinot Noir, she was having difficulty keeping her big blue eyes open. It was 1a.m. according to the alarm clock on Conor's night stand. The black-haired blade was fast asleep and snoring lightly. Her shop opened at nine but she liked to get there an hour early, make sure the day could begin without a crinkle. Also, if someone were to call in sick, there would be a message on the office machine and she'd have time to call round a trusted roster of folks looking for stopgap work.

She had to go. She was grateful for the chance to feel desirable again but, for women of her sort, life revolved around work. She had plans to expand and had already made a bid on a location in West Seattle. She stroked Conor's cheek and gave him a light peck goodbye before searching in the dark for her shoes and clothes.

She retrieved a notepad from her purse but was nonplussed: what do you say to a sexy young man who just boffed your Botox out? 'Good luck with your studies!' seemed ridiculous as did 'Thanks for the pizza!' She settled on 'I had a wonderful time – xox, Delta.'

She called a cab and reached her condo in Queen Anne where she tumbled into her own bed to catch four or five hours of fitful sleep.

A dream woke her out of a reverie long before the alarm buzzed. She and Conor had just enjoyed marathon sex. She was going down on him in what she hoped to be a prelude to more marathon sex. She interrupted her role as fellatrix to sit in Conor's lap and say, 'I've waited all my life to feel like this.' Then she parachuted back to where she needed to be.

She woke up shaking her head. What a crazy dream! She was blessed – or cursed – with the ability to always remember her dreams. Well, this one would have to remain tucked like a sheet with hospital corners into her subconscious because she had no intention of repeating last night's encounter. Why set oneself up to play the fool?

Not bothering to wait for the alarm, she brewed a pot of coffee and set her workaday wheels in motion. I'll just bake that man right out of my hair, she said to herself with a chuckle.

Business was brisk that day and Delta managed to stay focused, envisioning Conor's naked torso only a few hundred times.

When she got home that night, she sat down at her computer and willed herself not to turn it on. She put on a CD, poured a glass of wine and flipped through some magazines. It was no use; her mind kept circling back to the monitor with its persistent Turn Me On button.

So she plugged into cyberspace to revisit Conor's ad. It was gone. Well, that didn't mean anything. A guy that handsome could easily pick someone up at a bar, though he told her he wasn't into the bar scene.

On Mondays she opened the shop at noon and closed later in the evening. She had just thanked her last customer and put out a CLOSED sign when she saw a familiar gallant figure striding through her humble establishment.

He was carrying a bouquet of flowers. He dropped it, picked her up by the waist and swung her round like a girl at a rodeo.

She laughed and curled into his embrace.

'Let me show you my office,' she said, grabbing him by the sleeve of his fleece jacket. She didn't care about the age difference anymore. She was as young as he wanted her to be. They could have been lovers on a beach, tugging hearts like kites on a string.

'I didn't expect to see you again,' she said, unzipping his fly.

'I gathered that by the laconic note you left. At least you didn't write, "Thanks for the pizza" and skedaddle. An "xox" gives a guy reason to hope.'

She had his cock in her hand and was about to suck it like a lozenge when he pressed her to the wall and took her face in his hands.

'You have to let me kiss you before you do that,' he said. His mouth covered hers and she melted; she could feel liquid sensations dropping from her thorax through her abdomen and past her sex until they reached the spaces between her tingling toes.

She had found someone who made her *tingle*; that was a first and it didn't feel silly. It felt wholly and completely necessary.

It also felt necessary to fuck like nymph and satyr in some primordial forest of love. She guided her young lover to an ergonomic chair, apologising for the material that was sure to chafe his bum. What followed next would hopefully take his mind off any discomfort.

From the moment her tongue lazed round the tip of his cock, she was wetter than she had ever been. When her lips engulfed his cock like gift wrap she was squirming with desire. She could have sucked him until it was time to open the shop again in the morning but there he was pulling her up, filling her moist mound with his fingers and guiding her torso in a prime fucking position.

'Guess you don't need lube,' he mused, with a smile as big as the sun.

'No,' Delta agreed. 'I need you inside me.'

He kissed her again before she straddled his cock, holding on to the back of the chair as he fucked her into a happier realm, fucked her into that primordial forest where wetness and dew lined every tree, every blade of grass.

Her world expanded with every thrust and he held fast to her spine as she arched her back for a rip-snorting come.

'Oh, Conor. Conor, what are we doing?' It was a few minutes before she could go vertical after the finale of their chair humping. Now Delta was standing, peering through a space in her venetian blinds. Good thing she had remembered to lock the door.

She spun around and said, 'This is crazy.'

'Why is it crazy?' Conor asked, running a hand along her exposed thigh.

'It can't lead to anything,' she reasoned, not meeting his eye. From the core of her heart, she didn't want this to be true.

'You don't know that,' he said, giving her a reassuring hug and a kiss to go with it. 'Look, I won't deny I was looking for something casual. So were you. But we found each other and there's obviously a connection here. Let's see where it goes.'

Delta smiled at him. He bestowed the look of an earnest scholar even after surviving an older woman's fit of ardour.

'Right now I need to go home; I haven't eaten anything all day. No need to point out the irony of a crumpet-shop purveyor going hungry. I'm just so busy serving and totting up accounts, there's no time for a bite. I sure wouldn't mind nibbling on you a little more, sweetness.'

Delta and Conor left the shop. From that point on they'd both find crumbs in their sheets because no one could resist Delta May Crane's crumpets, especially when propped against a palisade of pillows while watching late-night movies.

But there were no more goodbye notes. Every day the lovers found new ways to say hello.

Things to Do in New York When It's 90
Chrissie Bentley

Crouching over Debbie's expectant face, I parted the lips of my pussy and watched the come hang suspended for a moment, before falling heavily into her open mouth.

She closed her lips, and moaned delightedly. 'Oh, Chrissie! You have to try this!'

I bent to kiss her mouth, as she made an offering on the tip of her tongue. Then I felt myself hurtling forward, as she grabbed my ass and pulled my still dripping cunt towards her mouth. I glanced at Martin, propped up on one arm alongside us, watching as he recovered from the fucking he'd just given me. Poor boy, he might as well go home now. We had no further use for him.

* * *

How sick are you of hearing about the heatwave? It's August on the East Coast, folks. Buy yourself an icepack. At least, that's what I said yesterday at work, when the inevitable round of whining kicked up ('Oh, when are we going to get some relief from this awful weather?').

I felt a little different this morning, when I woke up just in time to hear the dreadful clunk of the electricity going down, and the last despairing groan of the air conditioning. And when I called the building's super just before I left work, and he told me that the power was still out, well, as Debbie put it when I walked past her desk, 'Bet you don't feel quite so smug now, do you?'

We chatted for a moment. Well, she chatted. I whined. 'So why don't you come over to my place?' she suggested. She'd already checked with a neighbour; their power was still up and running and, even if it did go out, she had bedrooms and a family room in the basement. 'And it's always plenty cool down there.'

I nodded my thanks, as she rose and called out to the rest of the office, 'Anyone else need some place to hang out?'

A couple of people looked tempted, but Martin was the only one who said yes, which suited me fine. So what if I was still newly married the year he was born, and divorced by the time he left high school? I've always put my faith in chemistry, not chronology, and so what if he was still wet behind the ears? A couple of work

114

Christmas parties ago, he got me wetter in a lot more places than that. We'd never repeated that one night together, but he had become one of those co-workers I always had time for, and the feeling had always been mutual. Oh, and he had the hots for Debbie; him and every other guy in the office.

Debbie, on the other hand, never seemed to get the hots for anyone. We'd often gone out for a drink after work and, I swear, the woman wasn't simply married to her job, she was having an affair with it as well. I wondered what her house looked like; I knew she'd inherited it from her parents, and I had always visualised it as one of those 1950s ranches that dominate the suburbs. And, give or take a couple of floors, the odd Gothic tower and a yard that made the Munsters look house-proud, I was right.

She ushered us in, apologised for the mess and ran to the refrigerator. 'Pizza good for you both? Beer, wine, soda? Great. Half an hour till we eat.'

She handed round our drinks and led us into the living room, swept a few papers (I recognised the letterhead; it was all work stuff) off the sofa and then glanced apologetically at the TV. 'Sorry, I never bothered getting cable. Hardly ever have time to watch the thing, anyway.'

'Oh shit, does that mean we have to talk to one another?' Martin said with mock horror. He raised his wine glass. 'I hope you've got plenty of this stuff on hand.'

Debbie laughed. 'Don't worry, I stocked up at the weekend.' The thought crossed my mind: is this what she does every night, sit around doing overtime and glugging her way through a few bottles of wine? No wonder she always looked so cheerful.

She read my mind. 'It's OK, I'm strictly a one-glass-a-night girl. But you never know when people are going to drop by,' and she said it as though that was how she really spent her time, throwing open her doors to a phonebook full of friends. I guess she really enjoys talking to people.

She was right. She certainly had stocked up. We'd sunk three bottles before we'd even finished eating, and, whenever one looked even two-thirds empty, she'd be up to grab another. Conversation, on the other hand, was – I think 'odd' is the word for it. The more Martin drank, the more tongue-tied he seemed to become, but that was understandable. He'd been desperate to get into Debbie's pants for so long that simply sharing the sofa with her must have made him feel like he was halfway there. And Debbie had something on her mind as well, but we'd switched from white wine to red before she let on what it was.

'So, you two at the last but one Christmas party.'

I laughed aloud. 'Were we that obvious?'

'When do you mean?' she asked. 'Before you disappeared into the ladies' room for ten minutes, or after?'

'That was never ten minutes,' Martin shot back. 'It was at least half an hour.'

Debbie raised her eyebrows playfully. 'Really? Half an hour. Chrissie – what do you say?'

I was still trying to remember if it had even been ten. From what I recall, the cubicle was so small that we gave up trying after thirty seconds, and went back to his place instead. 'I don't know. Maybe not half an hour in there. But I think we made up for that later.'

'Go on then, tell.'

I looked over at Martin. His eyes were wide and he was shaking his head vigorously, in that strangely over-exaggerated way people do when they think that nobody else is watching them. Debbie, however, had eyes like a hawk. 'Come on, Martin, it wasn't that bad, was it?'

Now it was my turn to feel oddly defensive. 'Yes, go on, Martin. Was it?'

'Why do women always gang up on guys?' He took a long drink. 'I knew I shouldn't have come here tonight. As soon as I said yes, I knew that the two of you would wind up picking on me.'

'Ah, poor Martin.' Debbie draped an arm around his shoulder. 'Tell mommy all about it.'

I smiled, because at that moment she did look almost maternal, and again I thought about my own mating motto. Chemistry not chronology. Well, they certainly had that.

117

Debbie glanced towards me, her expression clearly asking my permission to continue. I smiled reassuringly. One night, eighteen months ago; it was scarcely a binding contract, was it? Martin, meanwhile, had turned so alarmingly crimson that it was worth watching Debbie paw at him, simply to see which would explode first. His head? Or his balls?

Debbie clearly had the same idea, running a fingertip down his chest, teasing around the buttons of his shirt. I wondered just how drunk she was, and then realised, probably no more than me, and certainly a lot less than Martin. He'd practically polished that last bottle off on his own.

'Hey, Chrissie, what do you say? Should Martin volunteer to tell me all the sordid details? Or should the two of us tickle them out of him?'

Martin squirmed out of her grasp, the confusion on his face reminding me of just how young twenty-one, twenty-two, really is. 'Hang on, this isn't fair. If you want to know what happened –' he looked around wildly, as though he'd forgotten where I was sitting '– ask Chrissie. She was there as well.'

'OK, I will. Chrissie – marks out of ten for Martin.'

'No!' he howled. 'No marks out of ten! I mean,' he spluttered as we both burst out laughing. 'I mean, you can't give marks out of ten for something like that.'

'I bet you do,' Debbie hit back. 'I bet you and your

little friends get together and compare notes. Girls do it all the time. So come on Chrissie, if "ten" is an orgasm that lasts all night, and "one" is a sticky hand and a box of Kleenex, where does Martin fit?'

Oh, I liked this girl; she reminded me of me. But I liked Martin as well, and I know how fragile men's egos can be. 'I'd give him an eight,' I only half-lied. 'Seven for performance, and an extra one for size.' There, that should please him.

'Ooh, an eight, and a big one?' Debbie was almost cackling now. 'OK, marks out of ten again. "One" is for dental floss, "ten" is for tripod. And don't just invent something to try to make him feel better. I can very easily check, you know.' And her hand fell onto his lap.

Have you ever seen the expression on a rabbit's face, just before a python swallows it? No, neither have I. But when I glanced at Martin, I had a good idea what it would look like.

'Come on, Chrissie, I'm getting impatient!' Debbie's hand was on his belt buckle now, slowly unthreading the strap.

'I dunno. A seven? Seven and a half, maybe?'

'That's your final word?' She had the belt undone now, and was fiddling with the buttons on his waistband. I smiled at Martin, who still sat frozen to the spot. 'I'm sorry, kid, I did my best. But it looks like she's going to check, anyway.'

'Damn right I am,' Debbie said softly. But then she withdrew her hand. 'Not right now, though. If that's OK with you, Martin?'

He nodded; not too willingly, I thought, but you couldn't mistake the gratitude in his eyes. 'She gave you an eight. What would you give her?'

'Oh ... er, definitely an eight,' he stammered. 'Maybe even a nine.'

Oh dear. I could see where this was going, and I had a horrible feeling that it would be me beneath the microscope next. The only saving grace was not knowing how far Debbie would be willing to take it with another girl. Or was that a saving grace? Maybe it just added to my predicament.

She swung off the sofa, and perched herself on the arm of my chair. 'A nine. I don't think I've ever had a nine. Or an eight, come to that. So, Martin, what does a nine actually do? What makes a nine a nine, and not a seven-with-honours?'

'I dunno. She just was.'

'OK, be specific. Does she scream and swear a lot?'

He shook his head, and she looked down at me.

'No I don't,' I whispered. Now I was getting bashful!

'Does she prefer to be on top or underneath?'

'Both ... either ... I mean ...'

Please, Martin, don't say it.

'We did everything, you know.'

120

He said it.

'Everything!' Debbie sounded triumphant. 'Absolutely everything! You fucked her tits? You fucked her ass? Did you suck her ass?' She wheeled back to me. 'Chrissie, spit or swallow?'

OK, that's enough. I was weak from embarrassment, but even weaker from laughter. I stood up shakily, looped my arms around Debbie's neck and pressed her face to my chest. I wondered if she could feel my nipples through the flimsy bra and not-much-better blouse I'd thrown on that morning. She should – they felt like bullets to me.

'That's a good question, Debbie. But I'll tell you what, why don't we find out?' I looked behind me. 'Martin, over here.'

He rose and, very uncertainly, made his way over. 'Now, how about if I tell her everything we did, and maybe a few things we didn't do, but we could have, and, while I'm telling, she can be doing. How does that sound?'

Martin nodded nervously; I released Debbie's head from my tit-grip, and her broad smile was all the answer I needed.

'OK, so we're back at Martin's apartment. I unbuckled his pants. Well, you've done that, so you're ahead of me already. And then I knelt down in front of him.'

Debbie slid to the floor, crouching on the backs of her knees, so that her head was more or less level with his knees. 'A little higher,' I suggested. 'Now finish undoing his pants.'

She obeyed, then pulled them down around his feet. His underpants travelled with them, and his cock hung bare, just a few inches in front of her face.

'Now,' I continued. 'You probably don't think that looks much like a seven, do you?' To be honest, I felt bad for the guy; I expected him to be soft, but he wasn't even making an effort. 'So, what you need to do, first of all, is pump a little life into it. Can you do that?'

She was still smiling. 'Oh, I can do better than that.' She grasped his meat between two fingers and raised him slightly while she ran her eyes over his helmet. 'Handsome little thing, isn't it?'

'Not so much of the little,' I cautioned her. 'Do this right, and it'll poke your eye out.'

'Really?' She leaned forward, and started rubbing his knob-end over her face, across her cheeks, against her eyelid. 'No, it would never do something like that. It's so soft, so sweet … you know, it reminds me of a piece of saltwater taffy.' She was giggling now, and her mirth was contagious.

'With a little button mushroom on top,' I added.

'Yeah, and I love button mushrooms. Especially in wine.' She reached for her glass; it was empty, so she grabbed the bottle instead, took a deep swig and sloshed it around her gums, and then very slowly engulfed the tip of his cock.

Martin gasped and then let out a long moan. I don't know exactly what she was doing to him, but I could see her cheeks working as her tongue rolled around her mouth; could see her jaw extending too, as the excitement rushed into Martin's prick, and he started to grow.

She broke away and took a deep breath. 'I'm still not sure about a seven,' she said thoughtfully. 'Maybe a six. Or perhaps I just need to work harder.' Her mouth descended again and wrapped around his erection, and her head started bobbing quickly up and down. I could see traces of her saliva clinging to his flesh, and felt myself growing wet as she gently popped him out of her mouth, dripped a great pool of spit onto his glans, and then stroked it across her face again.

'OK, now we're getting there.' She swallowed him again; almost literally swallowed him, her lips sinking down to the root of his cock, and only slowly releasing it from her grasp.

I jumped. Her hand was suddenly on my leg, and sliding up my thigh. I realised how wet – how absolutely soaking – I was, and stepped a little closer to her, as I grasped her fingers and drew them closer to my puss.

She glanced at me out of the corner of one eye, and her finger slid through the leg-hole of my panties and into my snatch. I moved again, willing that one digit deeper, praying for her other fingers to join it there, almost cried out in disappointment when her hand suddenly left me, and then yelped for real with pleasure as I realised that she was simply pulling down my panties.

Now she was inside me, two fingers, then three, pumping to the same rhythm that she was playing on Martin's prick – and suddenly four fingers, forcing me apart, back and forth, harder and harder. I opened my eyes; Martin was staring in rapt fascination, his eyes drifting from the girl on his cock to the hand in my cunt.

Suddenly I wondered, why are we letting Debbie do all the work? And then, why not? After the figurative tongue-lashing she'd given him earlier, how appropriate that she should now be performing the real thing. Besides, I had a ringside seat for the greatest show on earth, and I wondered whether Martin would give her any more warning of his approaching climax than he'd given me, that Christmas Eve.

He wasn't being truthful when he told Debbie we'd done everything but, in the course of that night, we did do a lot. His first orgasm was the one I remembered the best, though; after that, everything just blurred into one long fuck. But the tenderness with which he guided my face down towards his erect cock; the disbelieving gasp of 'Oh, God … thank you' that hissed from his lips as my tongue snaked around his swollen glans; the gentle roll of his hips as I sucked at his flesh; I wouldn't swear to it, but it felt as though I was the first woman ever to go down on him, and I wanted to make sure he'd never forget that.

I went slow, slower than I ever have before, fighting against my own excitement, to make sure that my every movement burned itself into his memory. It was magical, it was mantric; I moved like a hypnotist's watch, and he moved with me, rolling ... rolling ... rolling, and then, without a sound or a twitch or a flicker of warning, he was coming, and that was gentle as well, the slightest sensation of a slowly growing warmth, followed by the feeling that my mouth was suddenly filling. I continued to suck, I started to swallow, and only then did he make a sound, moaning aloud as he raised his ass off the bed in one tight, rigid spasm; a sharp cry and then silence again.

I released him and rested my head on his thigh. I felt a trickle of liquid leak from my lips and pool on his skin; my lips were sticky as his come dried stringy in the air. I gazed at the unblinking eye of his prick, as it lay staring back at me. A bubble of come leaked to the tip; I stuck out my tongue and lapped it up. I hadn't felt so content in months. Until tonight.

Debbie's movements were growing faster. I was coming, and coming hard. I rested my hands on Martin's shoulder, looking into his eyes as that express train barrelled down on me, and then down at his cock as my personal fireball hit me. I looked down to where Debbie's blonde hair still bobbed; I had never seen a cock sucked like that, with such grace and beauty, her eyes closed as she melded herself to his skin, and so completely in control. If she felt as good as she looked, she must be coming buckets – because I know I was.

My legs buckled and I crumpled against Martin, my breath coming in ecstatic gasps; and then he was clutching at me, as his cock flew free of Debbie's open mouth and spurted its own magic through the air, across her face, into her hair.

She fell back, looking up at me, parted her lips and let slip the first mouthful that Martin shot into her. Ah, spit, not swallow, I thought to myself, as I watched it pool on her breasts, and her hand rose absent-mindedly to run a fingertip through the goo.

I finally caught my breath. 'See, I told you he was a seven.'

Debbie's eyes flashed. 'At least that. And you're not so bad yourself.' She sniffed her sopping fingers as she pulled them from my cunt, then leaned across and kissed me there. 'Hey, Martin – play your cards right, and who knows what else you'll see this evening.'

He shook his head, as though trying to focus. He made a sound that might have been a breathless 'wow', and then collapsed onto the sofa. 'I'm not ready to become a spectator yet,' he said with a smile. 'You give me ten minutes and I'll be raring to go.' He cupped his balls in his hand as he spoke. Debbie and I giggled, then crawled across the floor towards him. 'In that case, I'll tell you what I want,' she whispered, as she lay her hand upon his. 'I want to watch you and Chrissie fucking, and then I want you both to fuck me.'

'I think we can do better than that,' I murmured. I pushed at her shoulders, pressing her down on the carpet; then, crouching above her, facing her feet, I began to slow-kiss down her body – her forehead, her nose, her lips, her neck, her breasts. I took a nipple in my mouth and bit down gently; moved to the other one and sucked hard. By the time I reached her pussy, as mine poised itself just inches from her face, she was as wet as I still felt. And, as her lips made contact with my screaming clit, I buried my face in her folds, revelling in the thick dampness, slurping her into my mouth and thrusting my tongue in as deep as I could.

And then another sensation, something knocking against the backs of my thighs; a whisper, a hiss, and then Debbie's voice, shaking with excitement. 'Brace yourself, girl, wonderboy's coming in from behind.'

Martin entered me hard, his entire length slipping instantaneously into my wetness, until his balls were slapping against my wet skin. Debbie was still down there as well – I could feel her tongue drift soft across me; could imagine her sucking at Martin's balls.

He was fucking me so hard that it hurt. No matter how wet I was, it was never enough to accommodate the cock that was now clattering against my uterus, so that every thrust, every breath, sent a sharp jab of pain shooting through my body. Yet, even though every nerve-end pleaded with me to make him stop, and my bottom lip was raw from biting it, I could not, would not, call a halt. Because always, at the back of mind, a little voice was telling me that it could only get better. And, when it did, it would be worth every iota of pain.

He was so deep inside me now, and he was still growing. I'd forgotten the pussy spread out before me; forgotten everything except what was happening inside me, the thick (and growing thicker) cock relentlessly pile-driving into my flesh, slamming harder and faster until my cunt was bursting and my body was tearing, and my subconscious was praying for him to come, even as I screamed aloud for him to last forever, for Debbie to stay forever, for the two of them to lick me and fuck me and hold me tight, and never, ever stop.

I was coming again, and again and again, three waves, four waves, just one after another, pounding me until I writhed flat against the body that still rocked and squirmed and suckled beneath me. The smell of cunt was everywhere, and that was driving me crazy as well – and then Martin came, with a roar this time, and a jolt so deep inside me that it might have dislodged my teeth.

I raised my head and prised myself off Debbie's sweat-slicked body. 'You OK under there?'

'Oh, Chrissie ... Martin ... that was amazing. I've never felt like that ... never done that ...' – for the first time all evening, she sounded lost for words. I knew what I had to do.

'Your turn, then. Spit or swallow?'

Her tongue ran long and hot against my thigh, sending a shiver through my entire frame. 'Well, I guess I usually spit.'

I licked her back. 'That's because you've never tried this.' Raising my hips, and crouching over Debbie's expectant face, I parted the lips of my pussy, and watched the come hang suspended for a moment ...

And that, I believe, is exactly where we started.

Dirty Gertie
Heather Towne

The house slept in the bright afternoon sunshine, high up in the Hollywood Hills. A hacienda-style, rambling ranch layout in stuccoed yellow and red. Home of Dix Akers, iron-haired, iron-jawed star of a hundred and one oaters from yesteryear. And his young firecracker of a wife, Felecia.

Dix was out on location in Gower Gulch, filming a Grade C six-reeler on the backlot of a poverty row studio. He'd ridden tall in the saddle back in the 20s and 30s, but time and changing tastes had caught up with the ol' cowpoke. Westerns weren't so popular after the war, Dix and his opinionated isolationist sentiments even less so. But he'd still managed to corral himself a new filly down Mexico way and, now that he was back north of the border, he was worried that the feisty young señora was cheating on him.

I slumped further down in the front seat of my baby-blue '42 Packard and patted my personal secretary, Malcolm, on the head. The eager young man with the mop of curly black hair and tight, toned, ivory body was down on his knees on the floorboards of the car, beneath the big white tilted-up steering wheel, licking my pussy as hard and as fast as he could. Superbly stroking this forty-five-year-old gal's slit and ego at the same time.

'Whoa, cowboy,' I cautioned the exuberant twenty-two-year-old, pulling up on his curls a tad. 'We could be here all afternoon, you know.'

He reined in his delightfully wet and wide tongue and looked up at me, his blue eyes sparkling, red lips glistening. 'You're the boss,' he agreed. He loosened his grip on my stockinged thighs and painted my pussy with long, slow, languorous strokes.

I groaned and tilted my dyed-blonde head back. Business was good in the PI racket after the Big One, pleasure even better.

I'd been in the war myself, overseas, pulling frontline nursing duty in Europe. And now, back in La-La Land, like most returning men and women flooding the sunshiny desert basin, I was endowed with an overpowering urge to make love, not wage anymore war. I was older than most, but still blessed with a curvy, busty body and audacious appetite and personality that attracted the young hungs like flies to a honeypot. I didn't intend on drying up anytime soon.

My pussy at the moment was a volatile mixture of Malcolm's warm saliva and my own hot juices. The young man had been working for me for a year, working my breasts and pussy over for half of that time. I'd taken in his hard cock on many a hard case. But with this kind of public stakeout, we had to content ourselves with a good old-fashioned pussy eat-out.

Malcolm pulled his petulant pink licker up in a long, dragging slurp over my bedazzled cunt, and then positioned the flexible tip at the top of my slit. He pulled his hands off my thighs, placed his fingers on my pussy and parted my swollen flaps, exposing my clit. He tickled the throbbing pink button with his tongue-tip. I quivered all over. The young man's oral skills, like my own experienced dick-tation, were wonderful.

I dropped the binoculars out of my right hand, clutched my tits with both hands and kneaded the shimmering mounds through my white blouse. 'That's the stuff Mama likes, baby,' I murmured, thrusting my trigger up against his tongue, jamming my breasts together in my bra.

Sexual fireworks were about to explode the quiet of that sun-seared suburban street, right out there in the front seat of that inconspicuously parked Packard, my clit and myself set to go off on the end of Malcolm's tantalising tongue – when, suddenly, another car sped into the picture and spoiled the erotic send-off. It was a black Ford coupe. It bounced from kerb to kerb up the street, taking out garbage cans and mailboxes. The clatter caused Malcolm to bob his head up, and we watched the runaway vehicle make a two-wheeled turn into Dix Akers' driveway and skid to a stop mere inches from the front of the house.

A man fell out, climbed to his feet. He was short and tanned, with glossy black hair that shone under the hot sun, the wax on his moustache melting. He wore a grey silk shirt and white silk pants, two-toned shoes. Through the spyglasses, I could see that his limpid brown eyes were as glazed as gimlets, his breath no doubt adding even more toxic exhaust to the already polluted atmosphere. I pegged him like a butterfly to a board as Lance Chalmers (aka Luigi Collocini), song-and-dance man, age twenty-eight, status married, notorious love 'em and leave 'em. He staggered up to the big red bat-winged front doors of Dix's abode and stumbled his way on through.

Malcolm crawled over to the other side of the floor-boards and curled up for a nap. My hotbox would have to wait, the case had just heated up.

Ten minutes later, we were jarred out of our lethargy by the shattering blasts of gunfire coming from inside the house.

Malcolm fumbled my pearl-handled .32 out of the glovebox and tossed it at me. I caught it by the butt, thumbed down the safety, smiled at the cutie, spilled out of the car. Just as more gunshots blasted the interior of

Dix's stable. I raced over the spacious yellow front lawn, kicked the doors open with a sensible two-inch heel and jumped inside the hacienda.

More gunfire, down the wide sawdust-strewn hallway to the right. There was cordite in the air, along with the faint smell of manure. I quickly sidled down the hall with my back to the wall, gun up in the cocked position. Past a watering hole, empty, the lid up on the toilet trough like cowpokes like it. Another shot almost took out my eardrum. So close – right next door.

Now maybe it wasn't my business to intervene, to fully throw myself into the case. But trouble was my business, too, and my client's homestead was under fire. So I curled around the open door like a sidewinder and stuck out my gun and cried, 'Stop!'

Felecia and Lance stared at me from the feathered bed of their lovenest. The pair were as naked as day. Lance was stretched out on his back with his head to the foot of the bed. Felecia was on top of the dude, cowgirl-style, silver .38 revolver in her right hand, caramel breast in her left, Lance's cock holstered in her pussy. There was a pile of shattered glass and splintered picture frames up on the dresser against the wall in front of Felecia, one 8x10 glossy of Dix with a bullethole between his eyes lying on the dun-coloured carpet.

Felecia had been blasting her husband's likenesses away with the six-shooter, as she rode hard cock on her lover.

'Who are you?' she squealed, dropping the gun and her breast. Her big green eyes blazed with unrequited lust, her lush brown body glowing with same. That rod up her pussy hadn't moved, Lance Chalmers a frozen rope inside her and out.

'Gertrude Flowers,' I honestly informed the adulterers. 'Your husband hired me to find out if you were cheating on him.'

The sprawled-out song-and-dance man sprang to life, grabbed Felecia's taut humps and tuned her tan nipples back in. 'You found out,' he said, grinning. He waggled his moustache from side to side, his compact body undulating beneath Felecia. 'Want to confirm it for sure?'

Felecia's eyes flashed. She licked her plush lips, and nodded.

I walked closer to the tangled pair, set my gun down on the debris-strewn dresser, my blouse and skirt down on the desert-tinted carpet. In the gumshoe game, sex is where you find it.

The twosome became a threesome on the wagon-wheel-headboarded bed. Felecia tumbled off Lance's cock and spun around, mounted his head, splatting her pussy down on his mouth, facing me. 'You can have the saddle of honour, since you are our guest,' the lovely *chica* allowed, pointing at Lance's gleaming horn. The guy murmured muffled agreement into her pussy.

135

For a small man, Lance was erected tall where it counted. That, and his swivelling hips, explained all his success with the ladies on-screen and off. I swung a leg over, picked up Lance's shooter and stuck it straight into my slot, and sat down on the pussy-faced man. His smooth tan dong glided inside me and almost right out the top of my spinning head.

Felecia grabbed onto my shoulders with her red lacquered nails, bobbing her pussy on Lance's mouth at a cantering pace. I bounced in rhythm on Lance's prick, the man thrusting up into me at the same sensuous speed. Felecia's pretty young face contorted into a bronze mask of wantonness, as she moved faster, rubbed harder. I thought Lance might suffocate, or drown in the obvious juiciness, but his pole briskly pistoning my stretched and sucking pussy told me all was OK; better than OK, in point of fact.

'Fuck her, Lance!' Felecia hissed, riding the high cuntry. 'Fuck her cunt!' She slapped my tits, spurred Lance's face between her knees.

I could see the guy's tongue flash down below, slurping at the moving, mushing target of Felecia's pussy. His hands shot off her humping butt cheeks and up onto her bounding breasts, mauled the exuberant pair.

I tilted my head back and moaned, letting my hair stream, my pussy take the wicked impact of cock churning tunnel, moving in unison. The bed creaked. Lance's muscled thighs smacked against my fleshy butt cheeks. The superheated air crackled with our impassioned moans and groans. This was the Wild West at its very wildest.

Felecia was the first to go up in smoke.

She screamed into my open mouth, yanking on my swollen nipples. Her golden-brown body quivered with all-out release on top of Lance's tongue digging inside her. His neck and chest flooded with her spicy gush.

'Hi-ho's, away!' I cried, surging with my own molten, melting orgasm, Lance's iron poker branding me with ecstasy.

I vaguely felt his come-gun blaze away inside me, Felecia's hot flapping tongue all over my face. The Dix Akers case had broken wide open in a stampede of unrestrained joy. Proving again that you just couldn't keep a horny young man and woman and seasoned PI fenced in.

* * *

I dropped Malcolm off at the office. We'd go over the case notes the next morning, in intimate detail. Then I drove over to a bar and grill on Cahuenga, in need of some food and drink to quell an appetite aroused by all my hard, heaving work. I was just coming up on the right turn into the Mussels & Francs parking lot when Max Toller suddenly cut me off with his yellow De Soto, drove me and my flivver into a back alley.

'Sailing that barge under the influence again, Max?' I demanded to know, slamming out of my ride to confront my professional rival. 'You need a driver's licence, not a liquor licence, you know!'

Toller was a big, slab-faced, slab-bodied punk in his early twenties, with a shock of red hair to match his fiery temperament. He didn't like 'dames' working cases, working period. For his age, he was as unenlightened as a fifteen-watt bulb.

He steamed out of his banana boat and banged up against me halfway. 'I don't like you snatching away business, Flowers!' he growled, glaring at my groin when he said it. 'Like that Dix Akers job – that should've been my meat!'

'Doubt if you could've handled it, sonny,' I countered, casting an equally contemptuous gaze down at his crotch. 'It needed a woman's touch. Or more beef than you could've brung to the rodeo.'

'A woman's place is in the home!' the guy grated in my face. 'Looking after her man's kids! Not using her T&A to take food off a man's plate!' He bumped me backwards with his belly.

'Doesn't look like you're suffering any, Toller,' I jawed, thrusting my breasts against his broad chest, bouncing him back a step.

'I'll give you something to feed on, Flowers!' He reached for his rod.

I grabbed his wrist before he could grab his gat, twisted his arm down and around, then up, spinning the big baby in the grey flannel suit. I thumped him against the side of my car in a half-nelson, hissed in his reddened ear, 'I don't like to be muscled, Toller!'

Then I reached down between his legs with my left hand, seizing onto a sexy idea I'd had for awhile. 'Unless it's with one particular muscle, that is!'

His cock swelled in my squeezing hand, to my satisfaction. The beefy young boy was getting the picture. 'There's room for both of us in this town, Toller. Room for what you've got to offer in my mouth.'

I'm a lover, not a fighter; either one if duty calls. There was no reason Toller and I couldn't get along, or get it on. I rubbed my large breasts against his wide back, undulated my pussy against his mounded butt, pumping his flesh-gun full of load. His body relaxed in my grip, all except his cock, which went raging rigid as a man can get and a woman can grasp.

I spun the lug back around, squatted down on my heels in the alley. Toller's normally angry mug was downright angelic now, as I deftly unhooked his belt and unbuttoned his pants, drew his dong out into broad daylight. My fingers could barely close around the thick pulsating tool, my palm clasping hard, hand shifting up and down the enormous length. This guy was truly packing. I popped his meaty cap into my mouth, packed it in warmth and wetness with my lips.

'Holy geez!' the big boy gasped.

His huge hands closed on my wavy locks, jerked my head forward, anxious for me to smoke more of the peace-pipe. I accepted the challenge in bloated inches, swallowing up almost half of his massively impressive cock. He bucked, banging back against my car.

I grasped his big, clenched butt cheeks and bobbed my head, sucking on his massive appendage. He didn't walk softly, but he sure did carry a big stick. It was smooth and clean-cut, pink and pulsing its entire length and width. I sucked quick and tight, deep as I dared, drooling out of the crammed corners of my mouth. Mama liked a raw serving of beef as much as the next hungry cougar.

Toller screeched, 'Oh, geez! Geez!'

His blunt fingernails dug into my scalp, his powerful hips bucking, his powerful cock blasting. The immature stud needed some lessons in control – temper and testes. He coated my throat with hot semen, spurting and spasming madly. I coolly and convulsively gulped like the tried and tested and thrilled cock-tamer I was.

When Toller finally flopped back against the car, his passion and prick spent like an LA flash flood, I pulled him out of my soaked mouth slow and easy and affectionately slapped his slit with my tongue. 'We going to get along from now on, Max?' I asked, cradling the young man's cock.

'Oh, geez, yes!' he yelped, putty in my hand.

I smiled. 'We'll still have our occasional "run-ins", though,' I promised the hunky hardcase.

* * *

It was just past six when I pushed through the doors of the Detmer Beauty Clinic on Sunset. I'd washed down Max Toller's surrender to common sense and uncommon sex with a couple of dry martinis and one wet, juicy steak, and so was more than strengthened to tackle my second case of the day. This one was special: I'd been hired by the DA's office to investigate Dr Detmer for possible unethical and illicit morphine prescribing.

I always like to get in good with the legal boys, and let handsome young Assistant DA Jenkins get good and into my pussy. The debriefing was scheduled for later that night, at his place of work.

Just as I strolled into the fancy clinic's well-appointed waiting area, a woman came strutting down the carpeted hallway from in back. She was tall and sleek and chic, with shimmering black hair and eyes, radically arched eyebrows, clad in more fur than an Eskimo. The wraps were mink, the woman under them Evelyn Lansdowne (aka Ewa Lewondowski), cinematic legend and legendary bitch-on-set. She was being escorted by a young, good-looking attending physician in a white smock, with soft brown hair. He was Gladstone Detmer, owner of the fashionable feel-good salon. I recognised his chiselled, cleft-chinned mug from the shot the DA had showed me.

'If you need anything else, anything more, just come back and see me,' the good doctor promised Evelyn Lansdowne.

She smiled magnificently and meaningfully at him, squeezed his hand on her arm. Her sculpted nose was back in its proper position, stuck way up in the air, when she sailed past me on a cloud of Eau de Paris.

'You must be Clara Button,' Dr Detmer said, clasping my one hand in the warm, dry, tanned pair of his own.

I was dolled up to look like the former silent-screen star who'd developed a career-ending case of 'mike fright'. 'Runnin' wild,' I responded by way of acknowledgement, tacking a coy smile onto the end.

Detmer ushered me into an opulent examination room, enquired as to what was bothering me.

'Everything!' I gasped, gulping a shuddering sob. 'N-nerves, I guess. I've—I've been so edgy lately ... and in so much pain.' I hitched up higher on the padded velvet examination table, showing more of my stockinged thighs. 'You see, I'm planning a ... return to the screen.'

Detmer's amber eyes beamed good wishes. He placed a smooth hand on my knee, squeezed good intentions. 'Your fans will be so excited.'

If they weren't already dead, I thought to myself. 'Yes,' I sighed out loud. 'But with these nerves, and all this pain ...' I fluttered a hand to my forehead in a theatrical gesture of hysterics.

'Oh, I think I can help you with that. As long as you help me.' The doctor's hand slid silkily up my thigh and under my skirt.

I stared into his eyes, licking my heavilyglossed lips. I'd applied the cosmetics with a trowel, as befitted a faded film star trying to act the ingénue all over again. My hair was curled like Clara's, my body needing not one iota of padding to pull off the deceit. I gently grasped Detmer's wrist and guided his naughty, unprofessional hand right in between my legs and onto my pussy. I moaned with intent, hamming just a little.

Detmer rubbed my bare sex with his talented fingers, expertly finding my clit with his thumb and giving it a good buff.

'Oh, Doctor!' I panted, shivering for real.

He laid me back on the examination table. He unbuttoned my blouse and unhooked my skirt, unwrapping me like the latest miracle medical procedure, letting my boobs and pussy loose. Then he bent over and kissed me on the lips, his hands exploring my breasts for symptoms of arousal, finding them at the stiffened tips.

I grabbed onto his head and mashed my mouth against his, thrust my tongue right inside. He was even less fearful of germs than he was of a malpractice suit. His tongue twisted around mine, pink and strong and slippery, his hands kneading my buzzing breasts, fingers reaching up and rolling my sensitive nipples.

This dirty doctor took the Hippocratic Oath to a whole new level – not doing harm, doing a whole lot of good – kissing his way down my face and neck to my chest. He piled my pliable tits together and sucked on the nipples, engulfing the straining jutters in wet warmth and sweetly tugging on them one after another. I arched up off the table, into his mouth. He pushed my glistening breast-beads up side by side and flicked his talented tongue across the stuck-out pair both together.

Then his soft lips pursed down my stomach, in between my legs, his wet tongue leaving a trail of electricity behind on my sizzling skin. And when he plugged his marvellous mouth-organ right into my juiced-up slit, I was jolted right heavenward.

'Oh, yes, Doctor! Yes!' I cried. This was the most exciting gynaecological exam any woman had a right to receive.

He lapped at my pussy, stroking me with moist budded satin. I shuddered with each thrilling drag of his tongue on my slit, jerked with joy when he pinpointed my clit again. He tongued my trigger to throbbing proportions, making me itch to get off. I dug my claws into his scalp and hung on for explosion.

But Doctor knew just what to prescribe his patient.

He lifted his head just before lift-off. Then he climbed right onto the table with me and pulled his overheated thermometer out of his pants and plunged it into my pussy. My temperature skyrocketed still more.

Medical ethics were left behind, as the sacred–sexual doctor–cougar relationship rushed towards ecstasy. Detmer swarmed his tongue into my mouth and pounded his cock into my pussy, hands clutching my breasts. I latched onto his taut pumping buttocks, dancing my tongue around his to the wicked tune of our raucous rumba. The padded exam table didn't budge an inch despite our banging bodies; it was obviously built to handle the frenzied weight of many such ultimate physicals.

'Oh, Doctor!'

'Oh, Clara!'

We spasmed as one, melding together in the white-hot furnace of blistering orgasm. His pistoning cock spurted into my sucking pussy, giving me burst after burst of good medicine. I hadn't felt so fine for hours.

Afterwards, it took Dr Detmer some time to fill out a morphine prescription for me. He used that time to develop the incriminating photos someone had been snapping on the sly on the other side of the two-way mirror in the fabulous examination room. They were his insurance, the bad doctor explained, in case I reported him for playing fast and loose with the pill pad and his patients.

They were also used to boost his fee from his married clientele by about a thousand percent.

In return for the wad of drug and blackmail money I handed him, Detmer handed me back a few explicit photos as a keepsake of my treatment.

* * *

Assistant DA Jenkins congratulated me in his office later that night. He was a tall, thin, distinguished-looking young man with penetrating blue eyes, porcelain skin and fine black hair. He was known for getting results, and I'd gotten him some, the paid-for prescription and pics, my sworn statement, fanned out on his desktop.

'Think there's enough here to nail the dirty doc?' I asked, leaning over the man's desk and showing him plenty more personal cleavage. 'I could go back, you know – for more.'

Jenkins' manicured finger landed on one of my black and white breasts in the photos, then rose to press into the in-living-colour version. 'No, I think I've got enough, Gertrude. Even if you haven't.' He added more fingers onto my beating boob, stroked.

'I can never get enough, lawman,' I murmured, pasting his mouthpiece with mine. As Lady Justice turned a blind eye.

A typically satisfying day for a 'dame' in the gumshoe racket – two solved cases and five studly men. Sometimes not all the time, but a lot of the time. It's a business that keeps a woman young, taking on all the dirty jobs and Joes she can.

Insegnante
Giselle Renarde

There was never money for piano lessons, growing up. All her friends got to take them – or violin lessons, or clarinet or voice or whatever they damn well pleased – but Sharifa was out in the cold. She used to pretend she wasn't poor, act like she was too cool for piano lessons. Better to be the bad girl than the poor girl. Looking back, her friends must have known she wasn't well off. Really, it was obvious.

But that was long ago. Sharifa was a grown woman now. She'd put herself through school on scholarships and part-time jobs, graduated with glowing recommendations from her professors, and quickly secured a position in business with plenty of room to grow. She had the condo, the car, the closet full of designer shoes, and all at the age of twenty-six. She was a grand success by anyone's standards.

Only one thing could make her life complete: piano lessons.

Sharifa bought herself a clunky apartment-style piano and signed up with Mrs Zamani, but progress was slow. She'd learned to read music a little in her school choir, but that was fifteen years ago. Plus, work kept her damn busy. Every time Sharifa stepped into Mrs Zamani's studio after a week without practising, she felt utterly humiliated.

Last week, Mrs Zamani had instructed her to rehearse the melody line of 'Greensleeves'. They would play it as a duet at the year-end recital, which was coming up in less than a month. Sharifa sat at the gleaming black piano bench and waited, but her instructor – or '*Insegnante*', as Mrs Zamani said – didn't join her.

'*Vas-y*,' her teacher instructed. The woman spoke at least five languages on top of her native Farsi, and used them interchangeably. It wasn't easy to keep up. '*Presto*, Sharifa, *baazi*! Play the piece.'

Sharifa took a deep breath and turned to find Mrs Zamani towering over her. There was something terrifying about a woman who was still so beautiful at Mrs Zamani's age. Her bleached orange hair was coiffed into a style that might have been avant-garde in the 1980s, but Sharifa thought it resembled Beethoven's hairdo in the portrait on the wall. Her skin was perhaps a shade darker than olive, much lighter than Sharifa's, and she wore make-up that was striking yet suitable.

And gold.

Gold on her fingers, a shimmering diamond ring, and gold bangles around her wrists which she removed and set on a tray before sitting down at the piano. Boy, could she play. Sometimes Sharifa sat beside her, taking in the dense spice of her perfume, watching those long fingers race up and down the keyboard like there was no effort involved. Her fingers danced across the keys. It was mesmerising.

But Sharifa had a sinking feeling she wasn't in Mrs Zamani's good books today. *Insegnante* grabbed a pointer – the kind an orchestra conductor would use, wood painted white with a cork bulb at the end for grip – and tapped the sheet music insistently.

'*Baazi*. Play!'

Feeling very small inside, Sharifa set her fingers softly upon the smooth white keys. She stared at the notes on the page and slowly plunked them out on the keyboard. She wasn't keeping time in any way, just playing the next note as soon as she found it. Mrs Zamani released the catch on the metronome, but that tick-tock sound only made Sharifa sweat. She was playing really badly. She'd be in trouble for sure.

Thwaaap!

Sharifa shrieked, feeling a sting across her fingers and wondering what had happened. Where had that whipping noise come from? Why was she in pain?

'*Ragazza impertinente!*' Mrs Zamani bellowed. 'You did not practise.'

All at once, the sting made sense. Sharifa turned to see her piano teacher brandishing that slim baton like a weapon and she gasped. 'Miss, you hit me!'

'Madame,' Mrs Zamani corrected. 'Not Miss. That was your punishment, *zibaa*. You must practise, or why bother coming to my lessons?'

'Don't worry, lady. I won't be coming back.' Sharifa packed up her sheet music in a huff, dropping papers, picking them up and dropping them again. She was so angry she could hardly find the door handle. 'I don't know who the hell you think you are, but doling out corporal punishment on your students? You must be crazy!'

Sharifa stormed from the studio and drove home way too fast. She tossed her sheet music on the piano bench, turned on the TV and grabbed a tub of Haagen-Dazs from the freezer. She tried not to think about Mrs Zamani or the humiliation of being rapped on the fingers. She tried not to think of 'Greensleeves' or the scent of her teacher's perfume, or the heat that passed between them every time Mrs Zamani sat down next to her.

Savouring a spoonful of rich chocolate ice-cream, Sharifa glanced at her piano. Her fingers stung with the memory of being struck. She thought about the expression on Mrs Zamani's face, harsh, but wounded, like a mother's disappointment. Sharifa had no idea her teacher took her progress so personally.

She placed the ice-cream back in the freezer, went to the piano and practised.

The following week, she tapped gently at the studio door and entered upon her teacher's instruction. She expected Mrs Zamani to say, 'Ah! So you've returned,' or maybe, 'You quit, Sharifa. You are no student of mine.' But no. With that slim white baton, *Insegnante* pointed to the piano bench and uttered, '*Setz dich*.'

Sharifa could only guess she was being asked to sit, and so she did, quietly spreading her sheet music on the stand. 'I practised,' she said, imploring some sign of affection, no matter how slight. 'I practised a lot this week.'

Mrs Zamani nodded, but her expression remained stone. Her eyes, lined in dark shadow, looked particularly catlike today. Like a jaguar, her ferocity was veiled in sleek feline mystique, but she was no less dangerous for her beauty. She reached forward, sending a gust of spicy perfume Sharifa's way, and set the metronome ticking.

Sitting so straight her back ached, Sharifa began to play. She tapped out the melody line to 'Greensleeves' without a single mistake and then, before Mrs Zamani could comment, she started again from the beginning. This time, she played the left hand too – Mrs Zamani's part in their duet. They were just simple arpeggios and she'd mastered them at home, but, with her teacher's eyes burning into the back of her head, she kept tripping up. She couldn't find the notes, even though they were right there in front of her. She struck the wrong keys time and again, slowing down, out of sync with the metronome. By the time she reached the end, she felt hot from her ears to her breasts, and so ashamed she wanted to hide under the bench.

She didn't turn around. Sharifa simply waited for Mrs Zamani to comment.

'*Vaay*,' her teacher said. Sharifa had heard this Farsi expression often enough to know it meant 'Oh, my', but whether that was good or bad stood to be reckoned. 'You have practised indeed, but you're not ready to play my part, *zibaa*. Not yet.'

'I played it perfect at home,' Sharifa replied. She wished she had proof. She should have taped herself or something. 'Honestly, I practised every day. I wanted to make you proud.'

Sharifa realised she sounded like a child begging for a parent's approval, but she didn't care. That's how she felt with Mrs Zamani. She needed to hear, 'You're a good girl. You tried your best,' or something along those lines.

Instead, Mrs Zamani said, 'Not so good, *azizam*. You must kneel on the bench. I will improve your performance.'

Gazing back, Sharifa caught a flash of bloodlust in her teacher's eyes and noted the woman's canine grin. Sharifa wasn't stupid. She knew that if she wanted to retain any form of modesty she'd have to leave now. But she didn't want to leave. She wanted to stay and find out just how far this jaguar would take her.

Climbing up on the bench, Sharifa kneeled precariously, setting her forearms on the piano's shiny black top. When she glanced back, Mrs Zamani was grinning.

She raised her baton and tapped it lightly against Sharifa's bottom. The taps were barely perceptible, but they sure sent a message. Mrs Zamani traced the tip of that pointer down the outside of Sharifa's thigh until it reached the hem of her skirt. Without a word, *Insegnante* pushed the fine fabric up and over her rounded ass. She gasped as the cool studio air kissed her warm flesh.

'How you can wear this?' Mrs Zamani asked, sliding her baton along Sharifa's black thong.

Sharifa shuddered as the pointer took its sweet time tracing over the pucker of her asshole. Even under the slick fabric of her thong, she felt everything.

'Thongs are surprisingly comfortable,' she told *Insegnante* as the baton moved between her open legs. Could that white wood tell how very wet her pussy was, just beyond the gusset of her underwear? 'You should try wearing one, see for yourself.'

Without another moment's hesitation, Mrs Zamani brought a hot palm down against Sharifa's ass. She jolted forward with the force of that spanking, nearly knocking over the still-ticking metronome. Even the follow-up slap came as a surprise – Sharifa had been expecting just a little tap with the baton.

'*Ragazza impertinente*!' Mrs Zamani growled. She sounded very put out, like she resented having to spank a student.

'I don't know what you're saying. I don't even know what language that is!'Sharifa whimpered as another blow fell against her ass. She dug her elbows into the sharp corner of the piano top, trying not to tumble ass over teakettle as Mrs Zamani issued yet another harsh slap. It had been so long, too long, and she'd forgotten how she used to crave this sort of attention. She'd forgotten how a dull sting could grow into a sharp burn in less than a minute. It didn't take much, just a few good smacks from a well-practised palm, and she was flying.

'Please,' Sharifa moaned, though she couldn't admit she was begging for more, not out loud. Oh, it hurt now. The pain was undeniable, and yet so sweet she hoped it would never end. 'Please, Miss.'

'*Madame*,' Mrs Zamani insisted, laying another hot spanking on Sharifa's blazing ass. The sting was so sharp she had to bite down on her arm to keep from screaming.

'*Madame*,' Sharifa repeated as she braced herself for another slap. When nothing happened, she gripped the upright piano and said, 'Please?'

The small white baton was back between her legs,

tracing up and down the crack of her ass, following her thong like a sheer black path. Every time that thin stick of wood brushed over her asshole, she seized, secretly hoping it would press into her, making room for a finger, or something even larger.

'*Setz dich*,' Mrs Zamani commanded. 'Sit down on the bench.'

At first, Sharifa didn't move a muscle. She didn't want to sit. Her ass was on fire, but she still wanted more. Finally, she turned her head and met her teacher's fierce gaze straight on. Boldly, she asked, 'Why?'

Mrs Zamani's cat eyes grew wide and her painted lips pursed. *Smack!* She struck Sharifa's ass unapologetically, leaving a needling sizzle in her wake. '*Setz dich*,' she repeated, spanking Sharifa once more. '*Baazi*! Play the song, both hands.'

The sleek black piano bench was cool enough that it soothed Sharifa's blazing ass when she first sat, but the effect wore off far too quickly. Her mind was so muddled from the spankings that her eyes wouldn't focus. Black notes blurred on the white page.

'Begin,' Mrs Zamani instructed. At least she'd spoken English this time.

'I can't,' Sharifa stammered. Her bum burned against the piano bench. The heat of her skin seemed to have penetrated the surface and she now felt as though she were sitting on a cook top. 'My eyes …'

That evil little baton came out of nowhere to snap against her fingers, and she jerked upright, so straight her spine felt locked in place. Without thinking, she began to play. She wasn't even looking at the sheet music, but rather gazing over it, out the long window overlooking the vast ravine behind Mrs Zamani's studio.

Sharifa had no idea she'd managed to memorise this piece, but she'd played it so many times over the past week that it must have taken up residence in her muscle memory. It was a part of her, and, now that she was concentrating on the blaze of her bum rather than hitting the wrong notes, she played it perfectly.

Mrs Zamani had never applauded a performance before, but she did this time. Sharifa's heart gushed with pride, and she turned swiftly to meet the pleased smile on her teacher's lips.

'And you said you don't respond to corporal punishment,' Mrs Zamani scoffed.

Naturally, Sharifa felt embarrassed to have been proven wrong, but she could hardly deny it. Instead, she lowered her gaze respectfully and said, 'Thank you for your help.'

Clutching her baton to her breast, Mrs Zamani bowed quite dramatically. 'You are too kind, *azizam*. It was practice that paid off, so simple.'

'Yeah,' Sharifa half agreed. 'But I only practised to spite you.'

A fetching gleam shone in Mrs Zamani's eyes as she took a step closer. The joy in her smile was replaced by something else, something more sinister. Sharifa's bottom burned against the piano bench. She wanted desperately to move, but she couldn't. Her teacher's predatory gaze locked her in place.

'Do you think I spank all my *studenti*, Sharifa?'

She hadn't really thought about it, but the idea made her flush. 'I hope not.'

Mrs Zamani's neatly pencilled eyebrows rose, and she smirked. 'Do you think I am a bad *Insegnante*?'

'No,' Sharifa replied, shaking her head. 'Not at all. Why would you ask that?'

She didn't answer, except to say, 'I reward my pupils as I see fit. When the children play their songs well, I stick a gold star on their sheet music.'

'That's nice,' Sharifa said, nearly breathless with strange anticipation. She found herself turning around on the piano bench, until her back was facing the keyboard and her front was facing her teacher. 'What about the adults? How do you reward them?'

With a casual shrug, Mrs Zamani said, 'Kind words, for some.'

Sharifa swallowed hard. 'And for others?'

Mrs Zamani seemed incredibly tall as she lorded over Sharifa, baton in hand. That Cheshire Cat grin was so wildly arousing that Sharifa's heart pounded in response.

She slid against the bench, slipped and reached out to right herself as her back crashed against the piano, bashing the keys. She was sure the cacophony would incur her teacher's wrath, but Mrs Zamani didn't react to the noise.

When the discordant music of Sharifa's fall died down, Mrs Zamani took a seat on her rolling chair – more of a padded stool, really. Sitting perfectly straight, she said to Sharifa, 'I have been *veuve* for almost thirty years. Can you believe that, my dear?'

Sharifa shuffled through her mental translation guides, but couldn't find that word anywhere. She shook her head. 'Madame, I'm not sure what that means, *veuve*.'

'Ah.' Mrs Zamani chuckled, clapping her hands. 'Ah yes – *veuve*, widow. I have been a widow since twenty-three years of age.'

The very idea gave Sharifa a shiver. 'I'm sorry. I can't imagine.'

'My husband was a brilliant man – intellectual, a poet – but he got on the wrong side of the Shah.' Mrs Zamani gazed over Sharifa's head and out the window. 'Now he lives only in memory.'

'I'm sorry,' Sharifa said once more.

'Shall I tell you a secret, *zibaa*?' Mrs Zamani asked with a keen smile.

'*Zibaa*?' Her teacher seemed to call her this at every lesson, but she couldn't fathom what it meant.

Mrs Zamani nodded deeply. 'Farsi,' she said. 'It means ... beautiful.'

Sharifa's breath caught in her chest. Her ears were burning with the pleasure of that compliment. 'A secret?' she stammered. 'Yes, please, Madame, tell me your secret.'

Wheeling her little chair close to the piano bench, Mrs Zamani leaned in and whispered, 'In all these years, in all the countries I've passed through, I have always been true to my husband.'

'You mean you've never ...'

Mrs Zamani shook her head slowly, side to side.

That couldn't be true. Mrs Zamani was so beautiful, so vibrant in her own exciting way. She didn't seem like the type of woman who'd gone almost thirty years without sex.

'Not with any man but my husband,' Mrs Zamani went on, slowly placing her hands on Sharifa's bare thighs. 'But no matter. In that time, I have developed a taste for *la chatte*.'

Sharifa could tell by the way her teacher spread her thighs that the woman was keen on pussy. It sort of bothered Sharifa, how *Insegnante* implied that licking another woman to orgasm wasn't on a par with fucking a man, but she set her irritation aside. She couldn't help herself. When she gazed at her piano teacher's lips, all she wanted was to feel them spread across her mound, that hot tongue dancing through her cleft, pinpointing her clit like an archer striking a bull's-eye.

Toying with the mechanism on her low little chair, Mrs Zamani descended almost all the way to the floor, stretching her legs out underneath the piano bench, pulling herself in closer. When she leaned down to kiss Sharifa's smooth thigh, her face appeared ever more striking, ever more beautiful. Her lips sizzled against Sharifa's skin like a brand, leaving shimmering roses of lipstick down the inside of each dark thigh.

Sharifa leaned back, trying not to let her elbows clang against the keyboard, but the strain in her shoulders was too burdensome. She let go and her body fell upon the keys for the second time that day. Mrs Zamani hardly seemed to notice, just staring at the apex of Sharifa's thighs, at the black thong that barred the path.

'Stand up, *zibaa*.' Mrs Zamani shifted to allow her room. 'Keep your skirt above your hips and turn around, my dear.'

Holding her skirt flush to her belly, Sharifa stood on wobbly legs. There was something about Mrs Zamani that made her so aroused and so nervous that her knees threatened to give out at any moment. She turned around swiftly, feeling quite bashful with her bum now shoved in her piano teacher's face. Leaning down, she set both palms flat against the bench. Her skirt hung down around her belly, blocking her view, so she was quite astonished when she felt her teacher's blazing lips against her ass.

'Madame!' Sharifa cried before she could stifle herself.

Mrs Zamani did not respond, except to kiss her bottom again and again, planting wet pecks on both cheeks, leaving traces of warm saliva to cool upon Sharifa's skin. When she whimpered with want, her teacher upped the ante, pressing the mounds of her bottom together and licking all over.

'Yes,' Sharifa hissed. Grasping the top of her thong, she twisted the black fabric until it brushed harshly against her asshole. Sharifa wrapped the material around her fist, stretching it, but creating a perfect burn against her puckered anus. Her clit benefited too, and not a moment too soon – it was throbbing between her pussy lips, pounding like it had a heart of its own.

Mrs Zamani dug her long fingers into Sharifa's flesh and bit her bottom indelicately. Those sharp teeth seized her skin, pressed incisively into her like a vampire, bringing a shriek up through her throat. She stifled it, biting her lower lip, squealing and squirming, but not so much as to make her teacher stop. She didn't want this torture to end – not now, not ever.

'Please, Madame,' Sharifa whimpered. 'Touch my pussy. Will you touch it? Please?'

The striking *Insegnante* traced a hot tongue all around Sharifa's ass, nudging one hand between her shuddering thighs.

'Yes,' Sharifa encouraged. 'Please, please, touch me!'

'Touch you?' Mrs Zamani whispered, her breath hot on Sharifa's skin. Pulling the black thong to one side of Sharifa's pussy lips, *Insegnante* moved lightly, dabbing her fingers into that throbbing swell, finding juice there and slathering it across Sharifa's clit.

'Oh, God!' Sharifa snapped her legs together, but Mrs Zamani spared no time opening them wide. 'Oh, God ...'

'*Khosh*, my dear.' Her teacher rubbed her clit while she clung to the piano bench, moaning with pleasure. 'Very good.'

'That feels incredible,' she said, trying not to move, trying only to feel. And then Mrs Zamani's tongue met her asshole, licking it through the sleek black fabric of her thong, and her legs trembled so hard she thought she'd tumble down against the piano. The very idea of her teacher licking her ass was so embarrassing her cheeks blazed like the sun, but all she could say was, 'Oh, Madame, please ...'

'Turn, *zibaa*.' Mrs Zamani slapped her on the ass, and she whirled around, stumbled, landed with a thud on the edge of the bench. '*Khosh*, very good.'

Before Sharifa's mind could stop spinning, her teacher's face was planted between her thighs, lapping wildly at her pussy lips, licking her pulsing little clit. Again, Sharifa fell back against the keyboard, sending a jolting discord through the room, but her teacher only snarled and ate her harder.

'Please!' Sharifa grasped at the piano, swimming in the keys. 'Yes, please don't stop! Please make me come!'

Growling like an animal, Mrs Zamani hugged Sharifa's hips and sucked her engorged clit into that hot, practised mouth. Sharifa couldn't help rocking against her piano teacher's face. Her pussy splayed wetly over *Insegnante's* mouth, coating those luscious lips with juice. That blazing mouth ignited her passion like fireworks, and once the flame was lit there was no putting it out.

Sharifa forced her clit against her teacher's mouth, rubbing it all over, getting herself off on a face that no longer scowled. In fact, Mrs Zamani seemed to enjoy being used this way. Was that a smile?

When Mrs Zamani pounced, trapping Sharifa's all too sensitive bud between her lips, there was no more putting off the inevitable. A blast of heat exploded between Sharifa's thighs, riding her muscles and blood to her heart, to her breasts. Even though she was seated, her legs trembled. She shrieked and hollered, banging her palms against the keyboard, which blasted ominous non-chords through the studio. She knew she was shouting, but what were the words? 'Yes, please, yes! Lick me, Madame. Eat my pussy hard.'

The shivers of lust blasting through her veins brought her to pulpy, panting glory twice over before she begged Mrs Zamani to pull away. 'It's too much,' she said, covering her pussy with both hands. 'Oh, I can't take it anymore!'

Her teacher laughed good-naturedly, though with a hint of something more sinister. Sharifa wished she could lie down, but there wasn't a couch in the studio – only a bench, and it was far too small. She was sitting in a slick coat of pussy juice, and the sensation embarrassed her a bit. Would Mrs Zamani make her clean up the mess? She couldn't picture her teacher cleaning anything, although before today she couldn't have pictured *Insegnante* licking her pussy, either.

'A challenge for the recital,' Mrs Zamani suggested as she rose from her low little chair. She fished more sheet music from her filing cabinet and handed the piece to Sharifa. 'Now that I know how much you can accomplish in one week, I don't mind putting your abilities to the test.'

Chopin's 'Minute Waltz'. Sharifa gazed down at the labyrinth of notes on the page, and then up at her teacher in disbelief. There was absolutely no way she could learn this piece in a week – maybe not even in a year. It was way too hard for a beginner.

Still, she read Mrs Zamani's eager smirk and imagined all the spankings she'd incur when she didn't get it right.

With a colluding grin, Sharifa said, 'I'll try my best, Madame.'

Money, Honey
Tenille Brown

If you called her a cougar or whatever hot-to-trot name the kids had come up with these days, Marie was liable to curse you out. She was anything but anybody's cradle robber. Marie was simply Marie, an older woman who happened to be married to a younger man, and who happened to still have the goods to keep his eyes right square on her.

Marie wasn't like other women her age. Not like the ones who had settled into the grandmotherly role, and not like the ones who acted too much like their own children.

She was one hell of a fuck and there was no denying that. They could go for hours, non-stop, and he'd be worn out long before her.

And she had settled down, as much as a woman like Marie was able to. At forty-three, she wore her shorts mid-thigh instead of barely covering her ass-cheeks. The wildness was in her naturally, always had been.

It was one of the main things that had attracted Gavin to Marie in the first place, that and her goddess-like body, of course.

She had grown up fast. She was out and on her own, working in bikini bars at nineteen. Marie had told Gavin the stories in one of these very clubs when she was thirty-two and he was a twenty-year-old college student, right around the time they started flirting and fooling around. She didn't give a damn about heeding anyone's warning, not her friends, not even her manager.

Soon after, they were an item, and, not much longer after that, they were inseparable.

Marie was good with her money, too. She didn't toss it around recklessly like the other girls. But she and Gavin didn't have that in common. Gavin was terrible with money. It slipped through his fingers like water. It was something he had never quite gotten the hang of, college-educated or no.

She had taught him the simple things, like keeping house and home remedies. She'd even taught him to fish! That was something his friends and family teased him about, especially his brothers.

Gavin grinned, for he wondered how much they would tease if they knew how often he eased her skirt above her knees and crawled between her trembling thighs. He wondered how many jokes they would have to tell about the way she massaged his cock until it was red, solid and throbbing, then took him hungrily inside her cheeks.

167

They wouldn't tease at all, Gavin was sure.

Yes, the passion he and Marie shared made them a perfect match in his eyes, but people on the outside looking in didn't understand that. People like his mother and his sister couldn't even appreciate it. They could only appreciate that once, many years ago, Marie had discarded her clothes for money.

But Gavin had married her anyway. He'd done it against his mother's and his sister's wishes because, well, he was in love with the woman and, though he hadn't had many relationships, he knew he wouldn't find the kind of love he had with Marie with anyone else, his age or otherwise. They had the kind of love you couldn't measure in time, age or money, so he didn't bother trying.

Didn't she have any real goals or aspirations about herself? His mother wanted to know, but Gavin didn't care if she did or if she didn't.

He loved Marie the way she was, working her shift at the restaurant and waiting for him until he got home.

He loved that, when he got there, she was usually naked, or wearing next to nothing while cooking dinner or dusting shelves.

* * *

These days, though, strange things were happening in their home, and even he could tell. Marie was spending

168

money just as fast as both he and she could make it, and that wasn't like her. And she was hiding it. The thing was, Marie wasn't very good at hiding it.

She thought she was, though. When Marie thought she was being slick, her eyes got really big like they did when he was fucking her (he loved when they did that) and she'd stretch her arms far behind her back and pucker her lips up for the wettest of kisses and Gavin would give her just that before squeezing her ass tightly. He could never bring himself to ask her about it – mostly because he didn't want to embarrass her, but partly because she had been there for him when he had no job at all.

Yeah, his Marie, she was something all right.

Gavin rubbed the hardness that was forming in his trousers. He poured a cup of coffee from the pot she had left behind for him.

He wondered what she had up her sleeve, but under no circumstances would he enquire before she was ready to tell. He just knew that, whatever it was, it was going to be good.

* * *

Marie was already dressed and staring directly into Gavin's eyes when he awakened.

'You're up early,' he said, and leaned in for a kiss.

She nodded. 'I want you to walk with me to work.'

'Then it's not because I'm getting morning sex,' Gavin said, but only half-jokingly.

Marie's answer was a smile. She leaned in and kissed him on the forehead, leaving traces of her lip gloss on his light skin.

Gavin furrowed his brow. 'That won't take any extra time.'

He dressed quickly. Khaki shorts and a polo shirt would do. He ran a comb through his soft blond hair before hooking his arm through the crook of Marie's and walking outside with her.

'When will your car be ready?' he asked her.

He pretended not to notice the bulge in Marie's eyes that revealed her nervousness straightaway.

'I don't know,' Marie said. 'Today. Tomorrow, maybe.'

But Gavin knew that it would be neither, not until he mailed the payment for her.

He soon began to notice her tugging him along an unusual path. 'New route to work?' he asked.

Marie tossed her head, her brown curls bouncing. 'Something like that,' she responded. Her short pale-blue uniform swayed against her legs.

He tugged at her hand, making her pause so that he could bend down and kiss her on her full head of soft, springy curls.

Gavin was anxious to see what Marie had in store, and he knew it had to be something. So he began to walk quickly, getting ahead of her and pulling her by her hand so that her walk became a sexy little trot and she had to tug on him to get him to slow down.

'Sorry,' he mumbled, smiling shyly.

'Don't be so anxious,' she said. 'It doesn't look good on you.'

After several blocks they cut across the street and Marie led him into a wooded area. She stopped walking just long enough to stand in front of him and kiss him on the lips, her naturally full set covering his thin pair, her luscious tongue sliding inside his mouth, slowly taunting him with its morning sweetness.

Then, a few minutes later, they arrived at their destination.

They were in the middle of the woods, standing beneath the biggest oak tree Gavin had ever seen, with branches that spread out a mile wide, it seemed. From the largest limb hung a swing with heavy chain links and a black leather seat. It looked out of place – it clearly belonged in a dungeon, not in the middle of the woods.

'How did you find something like this?' Gavin asked. 'Or *did* you find it?'

That was it. Marie had bought it and paid to have it installed.

Marie shushed him. 'You ask too many damn questions, Gavin. Let's just say … I happened upon it one day … OK?'

Gavin nodded and said, 'OK,' as foolish as he knew they both sounded.

'Have a swing with me?' She winked at him and walked ahead, peeking back at him over her shoulder flirtatiously.

So, maybe the car was gone. Maybe she had spent the money on some outrageous thing. Maybe he'd one day know what it was and maybe he wouldn't. But for now, Gavin thought, fuck the car, and fuck the walk. Gavin was going to fuck his wife in this old-fashioned swing that hung from this big oak tree in the middle of nowhere.

It took Marie only moments to get out of her uniform, to strip down to the sheer lavender bra and panties she wore beneath. She reached behind her back and unhooked the large cups that held her full breasts, smiling and keeping her eyes on Gavin as she did so.

Next, she helped him out of his clothes, unbuttoning his polo shirt first and pulling it over his head. She threw it onto the dew-moistened grass. Then she unbuckled his belt and slipped it swiftly through the loops. She loosened the button on his shorts, unzipped them and let them fall easily down his legs.

Gavin stepped out of them and kicked them aside. Right now nothing was as important to him as fucking his wife in this hardcore swing that was going back and forth, forth and back. He wouldn't have been able to describe the sensation if anyone had asked him to, but it started somewhere in the pit of his stomach and tickled him lightly in the groin.

Gavin had been a sucker for outdoor sex since Marie had introduced him to it years ago, and now he was mounting this swing, grunting and growling like an animal, hoping someone would hear them, wishing someone would see them. He was a sucker for having his wife straddle his waist, wrap her long legs around him and lean back, the momentum thrusting them forth, swinging them as if they both were young, but mostly as if *she* were much younger than she was.

Marie rolled and rotated her hips as she rode Gavin, as they both rode the swing. She knew just when to kiss him. She knew when to silence him as he was coming. He was sure to wake the small town they lived in, because, when he got off, he was loud.

She grinned when he came inside her. She clamped tighter onto his cock and then she came, too, clenching her eyes shut and leaning forward to suck a little on his neck.

'Good, baby,' she said. 'That was so good. I wish I didn't have to go to work, because I could do this all day.'

She hopped off of his lap, her bare heels digging into the ground.

Gavin stood and began gathering and replacing his own clothes. 'I suppose you'd better,' he said. 'You can't afford to miss any shifts, what with having to get your car back and all.'

Marie didn't miss a beat as she pulled her panties back over her hips. 'Can't get anything past you, can I?'

Gavin didn't ask for any more of an explanation than that. He was sure she had one ready to go, true or not.

He watched her walk away, on to her destination, before he turned to go in the other direction.

* * *

Entering their home after work, Gavin tripped over a shoe. He didn't know it was there. He didn't know it was there because he couldn't see it. He couldn't see it because the house was lit only by candles.

'Don't flip the light switch,' Marie shouted from the bedroom. 'It's a surprise!'

Gavin felt a familiar twinge of apprehension growing in his gut. Marie had been surprising him a lot lately, and it hadn't been his birthday, or their anniversary, or Christmas, or even Valentine's Day.

But, when he walked into their dimly lit bedroom, his lips spread wide into a smile. Damn, he was starting to love Marie's surprises.

His lips weren't the only thing that were spread. So were Marie's lovely long legs, all over their queen-sized bed.

'Trying to start a fire?' Gavin asked, only because he was nervous and didn't know what else to say. The candles were there. Scented and not. Tall, short, all different shapes and colours.

The sight of his beautiful wife in the buff still sent Gavin crazy. Natural Italian tan with tight cheeks and brown freckles. She lay with her arms folded behind her head.

'Something like that,' Marie said. 'Come here.'

Gavin stepped closer to the bed. Marie reached up and tugged roughly on his paisley tie, bringing his face to hers. He tickled her with his straggly five-o-clock shadow.

He climbed on top of her naked body. He breathed restless breaths on her full and firm breasts. He kissed one and then the other. He sucked firmly and fairly on her beige nipples.

Marie's hips rose from the firm mattress, taunting Gavin with the heat of her moistened cunt.

'Kiss it,' she said, beckoning him. 'Kiss it now.'

She coaxed him further by pushing the top of his head down in that direction and Gavin had no problem with that because, boy, did Gavin like to kiss it. He liked to look at it, too. He had to strain in the dimness of the candlelight, tonight, but that was OK.

Marie had a few strands of grey there in that rectangular patch between her legs. It was a turn-on like no other. He had never seen anything like it, hadn't known it was even possible.

He had wanted to ask a friend about it once, but was embarrassed. Women got grey ... D*own there*?

It was a foolish question, a boy's question, he knew.

But his Marie, she was neither ashamed nor embarrassed. She didn't try to pluck it, dye it or hide it. As a matter of fact, she let her legs fall open wider and pressed his head there harder.

Then she handed him a candle and gave him the OK. Gavin poured hot melted blue wax down Marie's sleek, milky body. She wiggled beneath the sudden sting of the heat and settled as it cooled on her naked skin.

Through puckered lips, she begged for more, and Gavin happily gave it to her until the small jar was empty and Marie's body was covered in cooled and dried wax.

'I'm ready for you now,' she said and beckoned him to her with a taunting finger.

Gavin crawled up Marie's body. Again she grabbed his tie and pulled his face close to hers for a passionate kiss.

She barely let him get out of his suit. He undressed in a hurry, tossing the garments onto the carpeted floor. Now he was as naked as she, and hovering over her, his cock inches away from her warm inviting entrance.

He had worked late, and Marie hadn't even scolded him. She had greeted him with a sweet reward instead, which Gavin found to be supremely odd.

How late was it, anyway?

He glanced over at the digital clock and saw that it was dark. He looked down at the cord. It wasn't unplugged.

Gavin looked outside and noted there wasn't a blackout either.

No, just inside their house was there complete and utter darkness, but for the candles Marie had set up to distract him.

Gavin sighed and carried on.

He'd ask her about the electric bill later, or maybe not at all. If he was patient enough, he'd surely learn her reasons.

* * *

She was watching him towel off, fresh out of a hot shower. Marie's eyes travelled the length of his white body, taking in his curly pale hair, blue eyes, thin pink lips. She always lingered on her favourite parts of him, his thick, firm fingers, his long, curved cock.

Then Gavin's eyes began to linger on Marie. Her right foot was firmly planted on a red-velvet-seated golden chair. She was wearing a black vinyl thong and nothing more. She was holding a purple silk scarf. Marie had something in store for him.

She reached down and pressed play on the stereo.

From the speakers came a song, slow and sensual. Her body began to move to match the tempo. She swayed from side to side, lowering herself to grind in an exotic dance. Then she rose back up, teasing her younger husband with her moves.

It was like watching her fifteen years ago. Gavin dropped his towel and walked towards her. Marie took her foot off the chair and nodded towards it.

'Have a seat,' she said. 'I've got something special for you.'

Gavin did as he was told, placing his naked ass on the velvet seat. Marie stood in front of him, gliding up and down and side to side to the music. Watching her expert moves, Gavin felt that nothing had changed in fifteen years. True, they had both got older. But you couldn't tell it from the way she moved.

Marie leaned back, way back. Her body remembered how it used to be when she was dancing and teasing for dollar bills. He had never begrudged her that, had never made her feel bad about the way she made her money. To Gavin, when she was on that stage, she was the most powerful woman in the world. She had a room full of balls just resting in her palm and all she had to do, if she wanted, was squeeze.

She quit, the day after they first kissed. Gavin hadn't promised her a thing. That was how he knew she wasn't after his money.

Marie smiled when she achieved her goal, when she felt his stiff-as-steel erection against the slickness of her thong. And, as she would have done all those years ago, she simply kissed him on the cheek and thanked him for being such a generous and loyal customer.

Then she cut off the music and sauntered away.

* * *

Gavin trusted Marie enough, but he began asking questions around town. After all, a man did have his pride. Both his mother and his sister had heard from Sarah at the cable place that his services had been disconnected for almost 24 hours before he had gone down to pay, and they had demanded to know why.

Damn it, he wasn't a little boy, and he wouldn't be treated as such. So he went down to Neiman's to see if his wife had made any big purchases lately. The answer turned out to be no, nothing more than a sweater and some perfume.

And he asked Helen over at Bergdorf's if Marie had special-ordered any suits or bags, but she hadn't done so much as walk by the department store in the past six months.

He suddenly realised that, since Marie had begun covering up her spending by giving him the most intoxicating and mind-blowing sex he had ever experienced in his life, she hadn't bought a single ridiculously overpriced thing.

179

It began to make him wonder. If she wasn't buying anything for herself, what was she doing? Was she buying something for someone else? Was she buying *something* else?

Out-of-the-way hotel rooms perhaps? Expensive dinners for a new boy toy maybe?

How foolish of him to think that a woman like her could be satisfied with just him for the rest of her life. Of course she was getting bored. Of course she wanted something new and exciting to tickle her fancy.

Dear lord, was some other man tickling his wife's fancy?

Gavin was pacing back and forth across the living room. He couldn't bring himself to go to work that morning, he was so upset with worry. It had all gone too far now. Was she ...

But there she was, coming through the door.

'Marie, are you buying cock?'

He walked straight up to her and screamed it in her face. He didn't care about her shock. He didn't care that she looked hurt. Marie was an older woman, a smart woman. She was good at playing on his feelings.

'Buying what?' Marie took a few uneven steps backward and placed her hands on her thin waist.

'You heard me. I asked you if you were spending your damned money on some fucking new stud. Now you answer me.' Gavin's face was flushed with rage.

He had never been an insecure man, not like this. The emotion felt foreign to him. He didn't like it at all.

Marie looked him up and down, as if he was a stranger, and stormed out of the room.

She returned just a few minutes later with an envelope. She dropped it on the coffee table between them.

'Open it,' she spat out.

Gavin hesitantly obeyed.

He found what appeared to be a very elaborate and very expensive fishing trip to Alaska, complete with lessons.

Gavin was speechless.

Marie was not.

'You should feel like a complete pile of shit,' she said.

He nodded.

'Another man, indeed,' she continued.

She took off her uniform apron and hung it on the coat-rack near the front door.

'I know,' Gavin said.

'How the hell could you?'She glanced back sharply at him.

'I know,' Gavin said again.

'I ought to slap the hell out of you.'

She drew her hand swiftly back to do just that, but Gavin grabbed it and pulled her to him instead. Then he kissed her, squeezing her ass, finally and silently agreeing with his older and wiser wife.

* * *

'It's not all about the money, honey.'

Gavin listened to the words roll off Marie's sweet little tongue.

She was right; it was hardly about the money at all. It was mostly about him and her, her and him, which was why they were mostly into fishing these days, rather than punching a clock and bringing home a check.

Fishing and making love, that is.

Gavin put his line down, reached over and did the same to Marie's. They could wait for a tug while he lay back and stroked the few strands of grey in her hair.

That sure was sexy. *She* sure was sexy, with her bare feet and long, flowing skirt. She didn't bother with a bra underneath his sleeveless shirt. She was always wearing his shirts, and sometimes his shorts too. Gavin thought that was sexy.

He eased Marie onto her back on the damp spring grass. Fuck the line. Fuck the fish. Fuck the money. Right now, he wanted to thoroughly fuck his forty-three-year-old honey.

www.ingramcontent.com/pod-product-compliance
Ingram Content Group UK Ltd.
Pitfield, Milton Keynes, MK11 3LW, UK
UKHW022301180325
456436UK00003B/169